I couldn't stop staring at him. On the surface he looked like a standard-issue student type: obedient hair, conservative clothes, shiny class ring and carefully controlled impulses. But his eyes were filled with emotion. I just knew that he was the boy for me. How I knew is one of the mysteries of life. Why does a lion look at a herd of antelope and pick one out? It was just bad luck that I had to meet him when I was sodden and had my hair dripping in my face.

"What's your name?" he finally asked.

I realized that perhaps I had been looking a trifle too long at his eyes fringed with long dark lashes.

"I'm Susy Howard," I said hastily. "This is my first day at HHS."

Books by Janice Harrell
Puppy Love
Heavens to Bitsy
Secrets in the Garden
Killebrew's Daughter
Sugar 'n' Spice
Blue Skies and Lollipops
Birds of a Feather
With Love from Rome
Castles in Spain
A Risky Business
Starring Susy

JANICE HARRELL is the eldest of five children. She spent her high school years in the small, central Florida town of Ocala and earned her B.A. at Eckerd College and her M.A. and Ph.D. from the University of Florida. For a number of years she taught English at the college level. She now lives in North Carolina with her husband and their young daughter.

Starring Susy

JANICE HARRELL

Keepsake
FROM
CROSSWINDS

═══CROSSWINDS

New York • Toronto • Sydney
Auckland • Manila

First publication June 1987

ISBN 0-373-88002-2

Copyright © 1987 by Janice Harrell

RL 5.1, IL age 11 and up

Dear Reader:

Welcome to Crosswinds! We will be publishing four books a month, written by renowned authors and rising new stars. You will note that under our Crosswinds logo we are featuring a special line called Keepsake, romantic novels that are sure to win your heart.

We hope that you will read Crosswinds books with pleasure, and that from time to time you will let us know just what you think of them. Your comments and suggestions will help us to keep Crosswinds at the top of your reading list.

Nancy Jackson

Senior Editor
CROSSWINDS BOOKS

One

Nobody at Miss Finch's School for Girls knew that I was only fourteen except my friend Esmée Crowder. I got Esmée to promise not to tell a soul because I hadn't been at Miss Finch's for long before I realized that survival was going to be hard enough even without the girls knowing I was the youngest. Luckily my survival skills were excellent, if I do say so myself, and in the four months since I had arrived, I had not only convinced everyone I was sixteen, I had carved out a secure niche for myself as the best blower of smoke rings in the dormitory.

I was demonstrating this skill as we sat around one night talking about Christmas vacation. We had posted a sentry by the door because it was strictly against the rules to smoke and just then there was enough smoke in the room to kipper a herring.

I exhaled a perfect circle of smoke, choking slightly as I did so.

"Nice," said Marsha, looking at the smoke ring unenthusiastically.

I sensed I was soon going to have to come up with yet another accomplishment in order to hold my slippery spot on the status ladder. "Going home for Christmas, Susy?" Vicki Hamlin asked.

"Yup," I admitted uneasily. I already knew that the reason Miss Finch's school always planned a ski trip to the Alps over the Christmas season was because quite a few of the girls didn't get to go home, and I didn't want everybody to think I was uppity just because my parents liked to have me around. "They're coming tomorrow to pick me up. I'm going to meet them at the station," I said. "I can't decide where I should take them to dinner."

"The Inn," said Pamela, who was lying stomach down on her bed, examining her talons.

"No, no," said Isabel. "It's gone downhill since its chef left. I'd try Grenouille's."

One thing we were all really interested in was food, and no wonder, with the two hours of skiing we did every afternoon.

"Not Grenouille's," groaned Pamela. "They'll get food poisoning."

"You were there the other night with Eric, weren't you?" said Isabel, looking at Pamela sideways. Eric was one of the ski instructors, and it was strictly against the rules to date the ski instructors. This discouraged nobody from doing it.

"I was," admitted Pamela. "The poor boy is looking for an heiress. I told him Susy's parents have millions."

Everyone looked at me. I presumed this was Pamela's idea of humor because though my parents work hard and make a good living, her parents are the ones who have millions. I think her grandfather invented the elastic that goes in underwear or something.

"Oh, drat," said Isabel, shaking her empty cigarette packet. "I'm out. Susy, would you go down to Liz's and get a pack of ciggies for me? She owes me."

I had the strong feeling that they were going to be talking about me while I was gone, but I didn't care. I much prefer that people talk about me behind my back rather than do it when I'm right there.

"Sure thing," I said. "I might not be right back. I'll probably say hello to Esmée while I'm down there." It was necessary to assert oneself somewhat at Miss Finch's or one could easily spend one's whole life going to fetch cigarettes.

I casually picked up a hockey stick on my way out the door. A girl named Robin lived in the room next to Esmée's. She was six feet tall and 190 pounds and routinely tried to throttle me if I ever passed her un-armed, so I never went in that direction without my hockey stick. As I believe I mentioned before, my survival skills were excellent.

I found Esmée alone in the room working on making an afghan. She had recently taken up knit-ting in an effort to give up smoking. "Where is everybody?" I asked. "I came to get some ciga-rettes. Liz owes Isabel."

"Take them out of her desk. She's out with Eric, I think. I'm glad I'm not rich. To have types like Eric panting in one's direction all the time would be a bore."

I recalled uneasily that thanks to Pamela's treach-ery I might be next on Eric's list. I thought I was pretty mature, but I had to admit that warding off a determined thirty-year-old ski instructor sounded kind of scary. Esmée put down her knitting needles. "Golly, just think. Only one day until break. I can't wait. I am really ready for a vacation."

"Me too," I sighed. With a sharp pang of antici-pation I realized how much I was looking forward to seeing Richard and Maisie and our cat, Heidi. I was looking forward to breathing a little fresh air in-stead of the perpetual smoke to be found in my dorm room. And I was especially looking forward to seeing Mom and Dad again and surprising them with how much I had grown up. After all, when I had left them in September I was only fourteen and now by sheer willpower, I had turned sixteen.

The next evening, I took a cab in to town to meet Mother and Dad at the train station. I waited on the platform as the train screeched to a stop, and I saw my mother step off the train with the long-legged grace she was famous for. The stationmaster, who was wheeling a dolly full of packages down to the baggage car, turned around and stared at her. Since Mother's career had been on the stage rather than in the movies, people didn't always recognize her, but they seldom failed to notice her because she truly understood how to make an entrance. Dad stepped down behind her, grumpy and with the unlovely profile of Abraham Lincoln. Dad was a producer, and he and mother never worked together, a fact that they credited for fifteen happy years of marriage.

"Mother! Dad!" I called. "Over here!" I ran toward them. I hugged Mother, burying my nose in her fur coat.

"Good to see you, kitten," said Dad gruffly, giving me a squeeze.

"The light out here is ghastly, my sweet," said Mother. "Your hair looks *gray*."

I touched my hair. "Moonlight Madness," I said proudly. "Do you like it?" I was very pleased with the pewter cast the rinse had given my normally honey blond hair. It easily aged me three years. With the rinse on my hair, I might have even passed for seventeen, except that I didn't want everybody to think I was retarded, being seventeen and still only in second year French.

"The taxi is waiting for us," I explained. "And I've made reservations at the Inn for dinner. I think you'll like their Coquilles St. Jacques."

Mother shot Dad a look. I decided they were probably amazed at how much I had grown up in a short four months.

After we got settled in the hotel, we went downstairs to the dining room to order dinner. Dad seemed rather silent, but then he is never exactly chatty. I looked over the menu. "I can recommend their Chablis," I said. "They have an excellent cellar for a country inn."

The way Mother was looking at me somehow made me nervous, and I groped for a cigarette in my purse. It never reached my lips.

Mother put one of her beautifully groomed hands over mine and the cigarette fell out of my fingers and rolled on the table. "Is that all you've been learning, Susan?" she said throatily. "Smoking, drinking, dying your hair. Darling, what has happened to you?"

I glanced uneasily at Dad and saw that he was doing considerable damage to his napkin, wringing its neck unconsciously in his hands. "Fourteen years old!" he finally choked out. He threw the napkin on the table and said, "I think we'd better have sandwiches sent up to the room, Maud. We all have a lot to talk about."

As we walked silently toward the elevator, Dad gasped, "Fourteen years old!" again, like a man about to go under for the third time.

I looked around me anxiously, afraid one of my friends at Miss Finch's was going to overhear this scene and that my cover would be blown.

Upstairs, we stepped into their room, and Dad closed the door firmly behind him.

"It's just a rinse," I said anxiously. "It will wash out. I don't see why you're so upset about it. Vera dyes her hair, Mother, and she's your best friend."

"Susan, Vera is a forty-three-year-old actress. She is not a fourteen-year-old schoolgirl. You must see that. Believe me, darling, if you want to celebrate your forty-third birthday by putting Moonlight Madness on your hair, I would be the last to complain. I'm afraid it's evident that you were just far too young to go away to school."

Dad snorted, "Dying your hair! Smoking! I can tell you one thing, young lady. You've seen the last of Miss Finch's. You're going home with us and staying home where you belong."

I was beginning to feel ashamed of myself. Maybe I had gone a little overboard in my desperate attempt to add two years to my age. At the same time, I didn't think Dad was being quite fair. Being at Miss Finch's, surrounded by all those criminal minds, had been no picnic. I deserved some credit for surviving at all. I didn't say that, though. When Dad's stern Puritan New England background started coming out, I knew the best thing to do was to keep quiet.

Besides, I was already thinking how lovely it would be to go home and stay home and not to have to worry about how to ward off Eric, the greedy ski instructor. I hadn't been crazy about Miss Finch's. In fact, I might have called my parents months before and asked them to come rescue me except that I had put myself in a really weak position when I had begged them for months to let me go to Miss Finch's in the first place. I had thought I would love spending hours every day on horseback. It had not occurred to me how quickly winter comes in New England and that horseback riding would give way to hours on the cold slopes. In no time, I got totally sick of skiing. Also, I had to admit that I did not find the girls very simpatico, and pretending to be sixteen night and day for months on end had been a strain.

"I guess you're right," I said. "Maybe I'm not old enough to go away to school."

Mother threw her arms around me. "My dear little girl, my darling," she said.

Dad was staring at the snow that was now swirling out of the darkness against the window of the room. "Smoking and drinking at fourteen," he groaned. "What next? I ask you."

I did think he was driving all this into the ground a bit. It wasn't as if I *liked* smoking and drinking. I had only been trying to fit in.

Also, I didn't see why he had to keep harping on my being fourteen. I would be fifteen in just a couple of months. I felt a change of subject would be welcome.

I threw myself down on the bed. "Oh, I can't wait to get home and see everybody," I said. "Richard and Maisie, and Heidi."

Mother was hanging up the jacket of her suit. "Cecily is coming home for Christmas, too," she said.

"Oh, lovely!" I said. Cecily was Mother's daughter from a marriage long ago to a stage manager who took off when Cecily was a baby and hadn't been heard from since. Cecily had silk underwear, beautiful fingernails and studied art in London. I had a complicated family tree. My brother, Richard, was Dad's son by his first marriage to a nice lady named Lydia who always wore a string of pearls and who had grown up with him somewhere in the neighborhood of Plymouth Rock. Back when Dad was married to Lydia, he had been in banking. Maybe because of that Richard was as solid and well organized as a bank ledger. In spite of this, I adored Richard. I had not forgotten all the hours he had spent playing Candyland with me when I was little.

Christmas was the one time our family all got together at once, though Richard was only with us a half day since he was at his mother's in the morning and Cecily was not altogether reliable about showing up. Sometimes when our whole family got together I would look around and think about how I was the only person who was related to every other person there. It was sort of strange. Strange, but nice.

"Have you decorated the Christmas tree yet, Mum?" I said.

"Oh, yes," she said absently.

Maybe because I was hungry and there was no sign yet of those sandwiches Dad had promised to have sent to the room, I was already thinking longingly of Christmas dinner. Since Mother was British and Dad a New Englander, our Christmas menu was an odd mixture of cuisines, but I liked it all. "Roast goose," I sighed, "chestnut stuffing, plum pudding, cranberry sauce. I can't wait."

"Hair dye," snorted Dad, still staring out at the snow. "Smoking! Drinking!" I sensed we were not on the same wavelength. I wondered how long it was going to take him to get over all this business. I certainly hoped it wasn't going to cast a pall over Christmas.

As it turned out, though, Dad didn't moan "hair dye" more than a few times on the trip home and I began to feel it was going to blow over, after all.

Two

On Christmas Day the apartment was looking beautiful, like something created by Charles Dickens for *House and Garden*. Bunches of holly and fir adorned the living room so thickly that it looked as if we had camped in a forest clearing, and by the fire in the living room stood the elegant brass greyhound, a gleaming contrast to the blue and ruby tones of the Oriental rug. That greyhound had always reminded me of Mother.

Mother appeared at the door of the kitchen bearing a roast goose. Since Maisie had Christmas off, Mother had produced the entire Christmas feast single-handedly. People were always surprised to discover it, but Mother was a first-class cook. She also could fix door hinges and beat almost anybody at Ping Pong. Mouths watering, we all watched her put the goose down in a place of honor on the table next to the chestnut stuffing.

Suddenly the phone rang and Dad leaned far over to pick it up. "Oh," he said, "and a Merry Christmas to you, too... Wonderful, I'm delighted to hear it," he said. "No, actually, we're just about to sit down to Christmas dinner. The children are home for the holidays, you know. Yes, yes, a very happy time for us all. Thanks for thinking of us."

He hung up.

"I guess that wasn't Cecily," said Mother.

"No. It was George Jenkins, the ass," he said.

Mother lit the candelabra and bore them to the table. "I can't imagine what Cecily can be thinking of," she said. "It does seem she could have been a little more specific. After all, what does 'home for Christmas' mean if it doesn't mean either Christmas Eve or Christmas Day?" She sighed faintly and sat down. "Well, now who would like to say grace? Perhaps Richard?" she said, flashing him a radiant smile.

He turned red and Mother, realizing she had embarrassed him, said, "Lowell, why don't you say grace today."

Richard flashed her a look of gratitude.

"Nonsense," said Dad. "Of course he can say grace. Go ahead, Richard."

Mother reached over and touched his hand gently. "The head of the house, darling. On Christmas, that's traditional."

"This shyness is a ridiculous affectation," Dad said crossly, "and the sooner... Oh, all right, Maud. 'Dear Lord, for what we are about to receive make us truly thankful.' "

Suddenly, I could hear the front door being swung open with a bang.

"Toodle-oo, people," called Cecily's clear treble. "I'm home!" She staggered out of the foyer laden with wrapped packages and followed by a weedy-looking young man with a feeble blond mustache. He was wearing paint-spattered blue jeans.

Cecily, who must have inherited her talent for entrances from Mother, dropped the packages on the floor and flung an arm in the direction of the weedy young man. "Dearest ones, this is Derrick—my fiancé."

"Good God!" said Dad.

Mother was the first to recover. With her inimitable stage presence, she rose gracefully from her chair and extended her hand to Derrick. I could not help but notice as he shook it that his fingernails were dirty.

"My dears, do sit down. I'll set another place. If only we had known to expect you!" She glanced involuntarily at Derrick's fingernails. "Or perhaps you would care to wash up before dinner?"

"Not a bit of it," said Cecily merrily. "We shall just sit down and dig in, shan't we, Derrick? The food on the plane was such swill."

Cecily, apparently unaware of the sensation she was causing, pulled up a chair and sat down at the table, while Mother set a place for Derrick, who stood sullenly by the table his hands thrust in his pockets.

"Well!" said Mother, when Derrick was finally seated. "This is such a . . . delightful surprise. You must forgive us, Derrick, if we seem a bit taken aback, but this is the first we have learned of Cecily's plans. Would you care for roast goose, or would you prefer ham?"

Dad was already carving the goose with an enthusiasm that could only be explained by his imagining that the goose was Derrick. I noticed that the whole idea of saying grace was dropped. It was very possible that at the moment my parents were not feeling truly thankful.

"Neither, thank you very much," said Derrick. "Cecily and I are vegetarians."

Mother cast a startled look at Cecily, and even Cecily looked a little annoyed at being reminded of this inconvenient fact while the fragrance of roast goose was wafting past her nose. She rose above it,

however, and said gallantly, "Never mind. We have
these marvelous chestnuts, don't we, Derrick?"

Derrick looked at the stuffing dubiously. "I say,
you don't happen to have any tofu burgers, do
you?"

"Fresh out of tofu burgers," said Dad grimly.

"Derrick is a carpenter," Cecily explained.

Dad brightened slightly at the news that his future
son-in-law at least had an honest trade.

"Not that I believe life is meant to be spent in
meaningless toil," Derrick said, helping himself to
the wild rice and mushrooms. "Cecily and I plan to
enjoy the moment. Life is too short to spend it
working, don't you agree?"

Dad began to look depressed again.

"Then do you plan to continue with art school,
Cecily, or...not?" asked Mother.

"Oh, I've outgrown school," Cecily said airily.
"I'm ready for Life. Derrick and I want to start a
family as soon as possible. We have our eye on the
dearest little hut in Sussex. And as I said to Derrick,
we can get all the water we need from the well, which
isn't really that far away. I mean, this infatuation
with running water is really a middle-class obses-
sion, don't you think?"

I could believe that Derrick might not miss running water. He seemed to use little enough of it. But
it was hard to believe that Cecily could adapt herself
to living in the Stone Age. I wondered if she had ever

tried putting on her makeup in a hut without running water.

I had been eating roast goose steadily while eyeing Dad's and Mother's face's alternately, as if I were a spectator at Wimbledon. It wasn't every day we had a family crisis like this.

"But, Cecily," Mother said, "even a little hut must cost something, and what will you do about food if you don't plan to work?"

"Well, there's always Cecily's allowance, isn't there?" said Derrick.

There was a deathly silence. Then Richard hastily slid his chair back from the table and got up. "Wonderful dinner, Maud," he said. "I think I'll just go work it off with a nice long walk. I can see you and Cecily and Derrick have a lot to talk over."

I was quick to take my cue. "Wait for me," I said hastily. "I want to take a walk, too." We both fled.

When we got safely downstairs, I collapsed in laughter. "Oh, Dad's face, it was priceless," I said.

Richard grinned reluctantly. "I know," he said, "but this is no laughing matter. Do you think she really is going to marry that guy?"

"How *could* she! He's dirty! You know how particular Cecily is. I mean, who else do we know who irons their panty hose? But at least it gives Dad somebody new to be mad at. He's been kind of generally crabby since I got back from school. Look at the way he was snapping at you at the dinner table."

We began to walk down the block with our hands in our pockets. We hadn't waited to search for gloves before we bolted, and it was cold.

"Dad can't help it," he said. "It gets to him to see me turning out like him. He wants me to be good-looking and charming like you and Maud."

I flushed.

"I don't think it's just that, Rich." I said. "He wasn't too happy about how I was getting along at Miss Finch's."

"Grades?" he said.

"Not exactly," I said. "He didn't like my new hair color. He also turns out to have this Puritan phobia about smoking and drinking."

"What have you been up to?" he said, giving me a baleful look. I recalled too late that Richard was sort of a Puritan himself.

"I've only been trying to fit in," I said. "That Miss Finch's is a jungle."

"Well, don't go destroying your lungs and liver, nitwit."

"I've given it up," I said promptly. "Anyway, you can see that the beauty of all this stuff with Cecily is that it gives Dad something else to think about. And I can't see her actually marrying the creep. Cec's a little flaky but she's not actually certifiable."

"She was wearing a ring, you know," Richard said.

"Oh, no, was she really? You don't think she can mean it?"

"It's occurred to me."

"How awful. Then he'd be a part of the family."

He sighed a little. "I hate to say it," he said, "but I don't like the way things are shaping up. I have the feeling this could be serious."

"It sure seems to be spoiling Christmas."

"It could be worse than that."

I looked at him suspiciously. "What do you mean? Do you know something I don't know?"

"Not exactly. But I've heard rumblings. Cecily springing this engagement on top of you getting in over your head at Miss Finch's—it could really make the difference."

"What are you talking about?"

"I don't know anything definite. Anyway, if it happens, it's soon enough then to worry about it."

Richard could be very exasperating. He was the original oyster. If he didn't want to tell me, there was nothing for me to do but pretend that I wasn't even interested. I also reminded myself that Richard was a pessimist of the deepest dye. Probably there was nothing to worry about at all. I didn't see what there *could* be to worry about except Mother and Dad being crabby and Derrick and his dirty fingernails being present at family feasts from now on.

We walked past a subway entrance. "When I grow up," I said idly, "I will ride the subway everywhere."

I had never been on a subway because Mother did not trust them. "So dark, dear. So unattractive," she always said. Even Maisie had to be picked up and delivered in a cab. Naturally Mother loved cabbies. "So resourceful. So colorful." Cabbies also loved Mother, who tipped like Diamond Jim Brady.

Richard looked at the grimy subway entrance. "If you want to ride on a subway, I think you'd better grab your chance now," he said.

I looked at him sharply. What was he hinting at?

It was easy to tell the family conference had not gone so well because when Richard and I got back from our walk there was no sign of Cec or her fiancé, and the cat was hiding under the sofa.

I didn't realize what a true disaster it had been, however, until the next day.

"Gee, it's going to be nice to see Angeline and Leslie again," I said, stretching out on the sofa. "I can't wait to get back to school."

"Perhaps you'd better give Angeline and Leslie a call if you want to see them. I don't think you'll be going back to school," Mother said.

"What do you mean I won't be going back?" I said. Visions of orphanages and reform schools began to swim dizzily in front of my eyes. I knew Mother and Dad had been upset with me. Was I about to find out exactly *how* upset?

Mother picked up a strand of embroidery floss and held it up to the light, carefully considering its color. "It's just that we plan to be moving."

"We aren't going to move out into the suburbs, are we?" I said. I considered that a fate worse than death.

"A little farther away than that, dear. What do you think of North Carolina?"

North Carolina? I was seized by a mad desire to go find a map. Not only had I never been to North Carolina, I wasn't exactly sure where it was. Of course, I had known one or two people who moved away from Manhattan, but they had always gone to Connecticut. In extreme cases they might go to San Francisco or Miami. Nobody went to North Carolina. "But how can we?" I said in a panic. "Are you and Dad going to retire?"

"Certainly not," she said a bit tartly. She had been getting sensitive about her age lately. "As it happens, your father has accepted the position of artistic director of the Phineas T. Philpot Shakespeare Festival."

My fingers clawed at a couch pillow as if it were a life preserver. "You mean it's definite?" I said. "We're really going to do it?" I was only now realizing how much I loved the city of my birth. Washington Square, Tiffany's window, hot pretzels on street corners—I loved it all. It was part of me. I was not sure I could survive if we moved away for good. I might be like one of those deep sea fishes that exploded if you took them out of their natural environment. Going to school in New Hampshire had been bad enough.

"Your father is talking to the trustees of the foundation right now. Of course, in the past your father and I have made it a rule never to work together, but we've decided we can't let that stand in our way now."

Mother's eyes took on a dreamy look. "I've been thinking for some time that I want to play the classics, Susy, and this is a golden opportunity. I've loved what I've done in musical comedy, but we have to face it that the musical is dying. If people only think of me in connection with musicals and Noel Coward revivals, I'll end up as dead as the dodo. I need a chance to show my real scope. I'm afraid that too many people these days think of me as a star and not as a serious actress."

I wondered when Mother had decided she had to play Shakespeare. Was it when Vera landed that plum part in *American Apocalypse*? That was the trouble with being away at school. You got so out of touch. If I had been at home, I might have seen the storm clouds coming. Richard obviously had suspected something was up. But for me it was a bolt out of the blue, a terrible shock. I couldn't believe we were really talking about moving away from Manhattan.

Mother picked up her embroidery hoop again. "But you mustn't imagine I'm thinking only of my career, Susy. Your father is looking forward to the challenge of the Philpot Festival. You know their first season last year was a disaster of poor planning and miscasting. He thinks he can save that theater. And don't imagine we're not thinking of your needs, as well. Your father and I are convinced that what we all need is to get back to traditional values and spend more time together."

"North Carolina?" I repeated numbly. "Nobody lives in North Carolina."

Mother gave one of her golden laughs. "Dearest, that's where you're wrong. The state is full of the most delightful people. And, of course, now that Richard is in school down there, it will be lovely to be closer to him and to see him more often."

I remembered then that Richard's school, Duke University, was in North Carolina. That information hadn't seemed very relevant before.

"What about Maisie?" I said. "I guess we'll never see Maisie again."

"Maisie happens to be *from* North Carolina," said Mother smugly. "It turns out her sister actually lives in the very town we're moving to."

I thought it was pretty low of them to discuss the move with Maisie before they even told me. It was a conspiracy, that was what. "Do I even get to know what town we're moving to?" I gulped.

"Of course, sweetheart. I think I have the name written down here somewhere."

She twisted around and began to grope through the slips of paper lying near the phone. Written down? I thought. She had to write the name down? I sensed it was not going to be a place that had a local branch of Bloomie's. It was probably going to be one of those towns like I had seen on movies with nothing but a filling station at the crossroads and tumbleweeds blowing down the main street.

"Here it is," she said, peering at a scrap of paper. "Hendleyville. Maisie is in heaven about it." She returned to her needlework. "The beauty of it is that it's within easy driving distance of the theater and the metropolitan area and yet it has the ways of a small town, the gentle people, the simple hearts. It's quite unspoiled. Solid values. I believe the town is quite a center for worldwide evangelism and has a well-known retreat for missionaries."

It was hard for me to see where my skill blowing smoke rings would fit in at a place like that.

"You said Dad was talking to the trustees now?" I said. "Maybe there's a chance the whole thing will fall through."

"Oh, no, dear. They've been *begging* him to come. They're very fortunate to get a man of your father's stature."

They were, I realized, very lucky to get Mother, as well, though she had modestly failed to mention it. Maud Weatherly and Lowell Howard at a single stroke. The trustees must be licking their lips.

"Your father only wants to make it clear that he needs a perfectly free hand and absolute authority," she went on.

"Then you think we're really going? Really?"

"Isn't it exciting?" she said. She snipped an embroidery thread with decision.

I felt sick.

That night Richard came to say goodbye before he headed back to school.

"You knew they were thinking of moving," I accused him.

"I thought they might do *something* desperate," he said. "They're going through a midlife crisis. Haven't you noticed? Maud took it hard that Belinsky asked Vera to do *American Apocalypse*."

"It's not Mother's kind of role at all," I said.

Richard smiled. "That's just the kind of narrow-minded point of view she's trying to overcome. You know *Chopsticks* closed a month ago, and Maud's not the kind of person who can spend weeks doing petit point. The move is a big step, but they've been talking about it for months. I think what finally made the difference is they've decided the kids are turning out badly." He grinned broadly. "You and Cecily did a good job of convincing them of that."

I groaned. If I could have foreseen this chain of events I would have been ever so careful to make sure I looked fourteen again before I had gone to meet Mother and Dad at the station. I would have worn a bow in my hair and knee socks, even.

"Cheer up," said Richard. "It could be worse."

"How?"

"They could have decided on Hollywood."

The next day I invited Angeline and Leslie over. We had a wake. Angeline and Leslie were very sensitive to my collapsed emotional state, and we did a lot of crying together.

That weekend, Mother and Dad went down to North Carolina to look for a house. I would have liked to go help pick it out, but I had been so depressed since the news of the move broke that Mother said that nothing would please me in my present state of mind. So I had to stay home with Maisie. I sat on the stool in the kitchen and watched her rolling out biscuit dough. "What's North Carolina like?" I asked.

She thought a minute. "Kinda backward, hon. Behind the times, if you know what I mean. But you're going to love it." She attacked the dough with a cookie cutter. I could not understand why everybody seemed so sure I was going to love it. I hated it already. I had decided I was the urban type, and right now I felt like chaining myself to the nearest skyscraper.

By the time Mother and Dad got back Sunday night, I felt lower than ever, but no one seemed to notice.

"We found the dearest house, Susy," Mother said as she hung up her coat. "You'll love it. And just a mile from the high school."

"The high school?" I said, picking up at once on the important detail. "What's the high school like?"

"The real estate agent seemed to think it was a good school, didn't she, Lowell?"

"I think it'll be okay on the basics," said Dad. "You have to keep in mind that it's not going to be as competitive an academic environment as you're used to." He cleared his throat. "You know, the Civil War and so forth."

I could not see what the Civil War had to do with it. That had been over and done with for a hundred years. "What's the name of the high school?"

"Why, Hendleyville High, I suppose," said Mother.

"You mean it's a *public* high school?"

Mother shot Dad a look that seemed to say they were moving not a minute too soon, before their daughter became a hopeless snob. I didn't think I was a snob, but I had never been to a public school before, and what I knew about public schools was gleaned only from the evening news where they seemed to feature teacher strikes, assault with a deadly weapon in the hallways and drug busts. I had a terrible fear that this move was going to be the biggest test yet of my survival skills.

Three

Thanks to the efficiency of Worldwide Movers, our entire household had been transported to North Carolina by the fifth of January. Even my old Candyland game, now squashed flat and with all the pieces missing, had been tenderly packaged up together with a collection of broken crayons and some dried-out magic markers and moved south. A few days later we followed our belongings, flying down and driving a rented car from the airport to Hendleyville.

Driving to Hendleyville, I noticed at once that there were certain similarities between North Carolina and New Hampshire. There were, for example, lots of trees. I personally had nothing against trees. I liked them, in fact. They were nice things to have around on vacations. What I questioned was whether we were intended to live permanently among them the way bears and squirrels do. I mean, if God had intended people to live in the forest, why did he create cities?

When we pulled up in front of our new house, I had the slightly sick feeling of someone who has gone down too fast on an elevator. The sprawling white frame house with the front porch and the rose garden looked like the stage set to *Morning's at Seven.* It oozed traditional values and Middle American normality. As far as I was concerned, that only pointed up the unreal quality of this whole experience. I wondered how long it would take for my parents to realize that we didn't belong here. I only hoped it happened before my whole life was permanently ruined.

A local crew had done the unpacking for us, and Maisie was already in the kitchen making soup when we arrived. Richard met us at the door wearing a Duke sweatshirt. He had taken the day off from college and driven up from his university to welcome us. "Nice sweatshirt," I said, letting my suitcase drop to the floor.

"I got one for you, too," he said. He held up a sweatshirt. It said, I Moved to North Carolina and Lived.

"Very nice," I said. "But a bit premature."

"Oh, come on, Susy," he said. "You're going to love this place."

It was not like Richard to be so bubbling over with good cheer. He couldn't be *that* glad to see us. I wondered what was going on with him.

I placed Heidi's carrying case carefully on the floor. She let out a meow as loud as a fire engine in protest, but I decided I had better not let her out until I had checked out the place thoroughly and made sure it was safe for cats. Mother and Dad immediately rushed in to inquire anxiously of Maisie whether any of our household goods had gone smash in the move. I cast a look around me. Our brocade chairs looked sadly out of place. As out of place as I felt.

"New girl in your life, Rich?" I asked.

He flushed, which was answer enough. In spite of my determination to drag the last ounce of misery out of my own situation, I could not help being happy for him. Besides having Dad's Lincolnesque profile, Richard had a constant battle with his complexion and in the past I used to worry that he would have trouble finding a girl who would really appreciate him. I was glad he had.

"Don't say anything to Dad and Maud," he said.

"I won't breathe a word. I promise. What's she like?"

"Very special."

"That doesn't tell me very much."

"It'll have to do," he said. "Enough about my personal life. I'll tell you what I'm going to do to make sure you love this place, Susy. There's a guy I know from camp, a really nice guy, who lives here. I'm going to give him a call and tell him to look after my little sister."

Oh, great. Look after my little sister. Talk about the kiss of death. "That's okay, Rich. Don't bother," I said, looking around me. I wondered what Richard's girlfriend was like. Rich was so close-mouthed I would probably never know. I promised myself that if I ever had a romance of my own I would tell him exactly *nothing* about it. It would serve him right.

Maisie appeared at the kitchen door with open arms, and I ran to hug her. "Hon, wait till you see your room," she said. "It's precious. You're going to love this place. I just feel it in my bones."

I felt that if one more person told me I was going to love this place I couldn't be responsible for what I might do.

The next morning, facing my fate as stoically as I could, I found myself standing in front of Hendley-ville High School. The school's architect appeared to have been frightened in his formative years by a trailer. It was made up of a collection of long rect-angular buildings connected by covered walkways.

Taken together, the brick buildings had all the charm of a penitentiary.

Large yellow buses were disgorging students over to my right. To my left cars and pickup trucks were careening into the parking lot and letting out more kids. I had asked Mother to drop me off down the block because I was afraid someone might recognize her and I didn't want to be conspicuous. I could have saved myself the trouble. In spite of my efforts I was conspicuous, anyway. All the other kids were dressed in Reeboks, T-shirts and old jeans. You could tell the girls from the boys only because the girls wore two tiny studs of pearl or gold in each ear. I, on the other hand, stood there in a long fuchsia sweater, black leggings and gypsy earrings that weighed four pounds.

With death in my heart, I found my way to a small brick building labeled Office. Stepping inside, I was immediately hit by a smell of damp sneakers, but no one seemed to notice the smell but me. Three kids dressed in Reeboks and jeans turned to stare at me as I came in, and I went up to the counter feeling as if ten rifles were trained on my back.

Immediately one of the secretaries came over to me, no doubt attracted by the bright blaze of my gypsy earrings.

"Kin I hep you?" she said.

I was momentarily stunned but reminded myself that this was English, even if it didn't sound like it and that I would learn to understand it in time. "I'm a transfer student," I said. "It may take a while for my records to get here."

"It always does, sugar," she said with sweet resignation. "Here, why don't you jist fill out this form here and I'll get you the student handbook. There's a map of the school in it, but I'll jist walk with you to your first class so you don't get lost."

I looked at the blank and was comforted to see that the printed word was the same both north and south. It was nice to feel on solid ground again as I filled in my name and birth date. I knew that when the secretary started talking again I was going to have to concentrate hard as words that I always thought were one syllable, like "map" suddenly acquired two syllables when she spoke and sounded like "may-up." I told myself that even my French teacher said I had a good ear and that I would doubtless soon pick up the lingo. The idea even gave me a certain morbid satisfaction. When Mother and Dad heard me talking like that they would be sorry that they had made me move down here.

It took me a while to work out what courses I should be in, and all three students had left the office by the time I finished.

"This is assembly day," said the secretary, "so I'll just take you to the auditorium and hand you over to your homeroom teacher." She glanced at my schedule. "You're going to just love Miss Ferguson for

English,'' she said. "She's a real good teacher. Everybody says so.'' As she spoke, I surreptitiously slipped the gypsy earrings off and dropped them in the wastebasket.

"Do I have to have my teachers sign anything?'' I asked. "Or am I as of now officially enrolled in all these classes?''

"What was that you said, sugar?'' she said. "I didn't quite catch it.''

I said it over again—slowly. "Oh. Yeah, that's right. You just show them your schedule if you have any questions.'' She looked at me kindly. "You're not from around here, are you?'' she said. "Well, never mind, I know you'll get along just fine.'' She led me into the auditorium and down the center aisle and showed me where my homeroom was. I did my best to shrink as we walked down the aisle—not easy as I am five foot six—and sank at last into a folding seat.

The assembly turned out to be Getting to Know Your School and featured introductions of all the members of the honor court and the student council. They appeared to be a very serious bunch of kids. A couple of them, I noticed, were in honor court and student council. *They* obviously had what it took to succeed at this place. I wondered if I did.

The rest of my day, as I went from class to class, followed a simple but depressing pattern: 1) Teacher issues book and adds me to the roll; 2) Teacher says he/she hopes I will like HHS; 3) Class stares at me.

What had happened to that Southern hospitality I had heard so much about? I wondered what would happen if I shook someone's hand and introduced myself. Would people faint? Would the riot squads be called out? First days are always long, I knew, but somehow this one seemed longer even than usual.

Storm clouds had gathered outside. I noticed, as I passed from class to class along the covered walkways, that it was getting darker and darker. I couldn't help but see it as symbolic. Imagine a play like this, I told myself, Act One—the clouds are rolling in and there is thunder offstage. You know right away Winnie the Pooh isn't going to come dancing out. Nope, it'll be witches stirring caldrons and mumbling, "Double, double toil and trouble." Storm clouds on stage are a solid indication there are soon going to be casualties among the characters. I had a feeling that I was going to be one of them.

When at last the final bell rang at three and all the kids streamed out of the brick trailers, sheets of rain were pouring off the buildings and a cold wind swept through the open passageways, catching my hair and making my sweater billow out like a sail. People were splashing through puddles in their sneakers, holding their books over their heads as they made a dash for cars and buses.

I had told Mother I would take the school bus home. But now I saw that there were lots of school buses, each with a number painted on the side. I had no idea whether I should catch number 19, number 21 or neither of the above. It was clear I should have researched the question more thoroughly before blithely assuming I could catch one of the things.

I stood there under the overhang, rain bouncing up from a nearby puddle to splash my shoes and my leggings as one by one the buses pulled away.

"Hopeless," I muttered. I took off my shoes and waded out into the rain. At least I knew the way home. I could walk. And with any kind of decent luck at all I would catch pneumonia and have to drop out of school.

It was unbelievably wet and cold standing there in the downpour. It was not just that my sweater and even my underwear quickly became sodden as I made my way out to the street, or that my wet hair was swept across my face, it was that I could hardly even see where I was going. The rain was bouncing off the streets and out of the puddles, making an extra haze of rain close to the ground. My clothes were sticking to me, and I couldn't decide which part of me was coldest or wettest. But in a strange way it suited me. Walking into a cold downpour exactly fitted my mood.

I could hear a car coming up behind me, so I stepped off the road, placing my bare feet delicately into a puddle as I did so. The car, however, instead of speeding by, pulled up next to me stood there with its motor running, the rain pouring down its sides in sheets. The door on my side was thrown open and the boy inside called, "Need a ride?"

I took a step away and peered into the car from a safe distance. It was one of the honor court-student council fellows. I recognized him from his being introduced in assembly that morning. While I was sizing him up, rain poured in a stream from the tip of my nose, from my earlobes, from my hair. I must have looked as if I had just risen from the sea. "But I'll mess up your car," I protested, raising my voice above the roar of the rain. "I'm so wet."

"I noticed," he said. "It's okay. Hop in."

I got in.

The water dripped off me, making dark blotches on the car seat and puddles on the floor. He handed me a handkerchief, and I dried off my face and fingers with it. It was nice to get the raindrops out of my eyelashes so I could see better. As for the rest of me, it was impossibly sodden. Noticing that I was shivering, he turned on the car heater and a warm rush of air hit my face and feet.

I told him where I lived. Luckily, I had memorized the address that morning.

"That's right on my way," he said amiably. "Hey, I'm Tom Brannen."

Now that I had got up so close, I couldn't stop staring at him. On the surface, he looked like a standard issue student type: obedient hair, neat and conservative clothes, shiny class ring and carefully controlled impulses. But his gray eyes were filled with emotion. I just knew that there was more to this Tom Brannen than showed on the surface.

I also knew that he was the boy for me. How I knew is one of those mysteries of life. Why does a lion look at a herd of five hundred antelope and pick out one? The antelopes don't seem to look that different, but the lion knows that this antelope is *his* antelope. It was like that. Kismet. Fate.

He was not the kind of guy that you normally imagine girls chasing after—slightly built with an intelligent-looking face and brown hair. But there were his eyes, gray and fringed with black lashes. Undoubtedly he was something special. It *did* seem bad luck that I had to meet him when I was sodden and had my hair dripping in my face.

"What's *your* name?" he asked.

I realized that perhaps I had been looking a trifle too long at his gray eyes. "I'm Susy Howard," I said. "This is my first day at HHS."

"No kidding!" he said breaking into a smile. "So you're Rich's little sister. He asked me to look out after you, but I didn't think I'd have a chance so soon."

I was vaguely aware of the sound of water slosh-ing up under us and of cars whizzing by in the rain outside. My hopes fizzled. All was lost. A bad first impression I might overcome, but to be thought of as Rich's baby sister? It was the double whammy.

"What were you doing in all that rain?" he said. "Couldn't you call somebody to come pick you up?"

"I felt like walking," I said.

"I guess it's tough at first," he said, at once sens-ing that a person does not wade into a cold down-pour with a song in her heart. "You miss your old school, huh?"

"Not hardly," I said. "Going to Miss Finch's School for Girls was like serving three to five for armed robbery."

"That bad?"

"I will tell you a story about Miss Finch's. This is a true story," I told him. "One time Isabel de Gre-ville's boyfriend sneaked into our dorm room and just stayed. Isabel brought the leftover crackers and rolls she was able to stuff in her pockets at dinner and the rest of us contributed slivers of bologna and a boiled egg, but by nightfall he was pretty hungry. Also he had torn his pants climbing in the window and had to sit around in Isabel's bathrobe. The dorm room started to look like something by Tennessee Williams. I kept pleading with Isabel to get rid of him, but she seemed to be making long-range plans. She said, 'Don't worry, Susy, I will bring him orange juice from breakfast. I will put it in this carefully washed shampoo bottle, which as you see fits handily in my hip pocket.'

" 'What would the Food and Drug Administration think of this?' I asked. 'What would the health department think of it? You can't mean he's going to spend the night here!'

" 'Susy,' said Isabel, 'not only are you a wet blanket, you are hopelessly middle class.'

" 'But what if he gets caught? What if *we* get caught?' I squeaked.

" 'Don't worry,' said Isabel. 'If the proctor comes in, we'll just dress him in that old hat I used to wear to mass and tell her my grandmother is visiting me.'

"Since the guy had an incredible five o'clock shadow and continually smoked these foul-smelling French cigarettes, I wasn't at all sure her plan would work, but it certainly gave me a burning curiosity to see what Isabel's grandmother looked like. I started thinking we had better plan for the guy's retirement. I was beginning to be worried he'd be staying for good."

"But then you got caught."

"Certainly not. Miss Finch's girls are never caught. As Isabel was fond of saying, 'No one with a soupçon of élan ever has to be caught.' No, what happened is, it turned out he snored. It only took one night until even Isabel was having second thoughts about having him as a permanent roommate. We tied some bed sheets together and lowered him out the dorm window during chapel the next morning. I was one relieved middle-class chicken, I can tell you."

"Sounds like Miss Finch's was pretty different from HHS," said Tom, grinning at me. "We're very straight around here. At least I think so. Since I'm a member of the honor court, I guess people don't tell me everything."

"This whole place is probably a sinkhole of iniquity, if you only knew," I said. I was pleased that Tom seemed to like my tale about Miss Finch's. Maybe I could woo him with interesting stories. After all, it had worked for Othello when he courted Desdemona and Othello didn't make such a good first impression, either.

Tom pulled the car up into our driveway and switched off the ignition. I could make out the looming shape of our huge white house through the rain.

"So you bought the old Burgess mansion. Like it?"

"Loathe it," I said, groping for the door handle. I was painfully aware that my lank hair was in my face again and that my clothes were sticking to me in all the wrong places.

"Have you ever thought about going out for drama club?" he said suddenly.

My hand froze on the handle. I wondered if Rich had been telling Tom about Mother. "No, no, I haven't," I said in a husky voice. "I'm not even sure of the way to the cafeteria yet. It's kind of soon to be adding extracurricular activities."

I did not add that I would have put raising poultry for fun and profit ahead of drama, if I had been looking for extracurricular activities. I did not care for the idea of people standing around saying, "Too bad the child doesn't have her mother's talent." Why invite comparisons when the only person you're likely to be compared to is one of the greatest living actresses? I looked at him suspiciously. "Did Rich say anything to you about me going out for drama?"

"Nope—why? Don't tell me you've already done a lot of acting."

"No," I said. "I've never done any acting." Could Richard possibly have gone through camp with Tom and not mentioned what Mother and Dad did for a living? Who was I kidding? Of course it was possible. That was Richard all over. The original oyster.

"Well, would you be willing to give it a try?" he said. "You'd be a natural for this play we're about to do."

I was interested in spite of myself. Working together on a play day after day with Tom, I would have plenty of time to overcome my unfortunate first impression, plenty of time to demonstrate my magnetic charm and my maturity.

"Are you going out for it yourself?" I asked.

He flushed a little. "Maybe. I've always helped out with painting the scenes, digging up the props, doing the lighting, that sort of thing. You know, just general handyman. Anything at all behind the scenes. But lately I've started thinking about trying out for Nick.'' He rubbed the side of his nose self-consciously.

"What's the play?"

"*Falling Star*. Do you know it?"

I choked, covering it as best as I could with a cough.

"Do you think you're catching cold?" said Tom. "Maybe you'd better get inside and dry off."

"I'm fine," I said, clearing my throat. "Well, actually, I do sort of know that play."

"Great. Well, then you see what I mean. You're a natural for Louisa. Believe me, it's uncanny. It could have been written for you."

Actually, the part had been written for Mother by Sterling Prentice. But Mother had insisted she was not ready to play the part of an aging actress, and Mina Simmons had been cast in it instead. We had gone to the opening night when I was eight. "No depth in the characterization," Mother had said sadly in the taxi on the way home. "Walks like a cow," Dad had rumbled. I remembered thinking even then that I could have acted the part better myself.

"Just think about it," said Tom. "Tell you what, I'll come by and get you for tryouts. When you see how rotten the other girls are, you won't be able to resist reading for you. Believe me, Susy, Louisa is *you.*"

I knew that Louisa was, in fact, Mother. But who could do a better job of acting Mother than I, who had been watching her my entire life? All I had to do was to use her mannerisms, the characteristic lilt in her voice.

I wondered if I could get away with it. It would be fatal to let Mother see me up there playing her. The very thought of getting caught at it curled my hair. If I got taken to North Carolina just for acting sixteen, I would probably get taken to Siberia for acting Mother as an aging star.

I could see it would be very risky. If I got the part, it would be hard to go to rehearsals for weeks without the parents realizing what I was up to. I wasn't sure I could manage it.

But then I remembered that Tom had offered to take me to tryouts and that this could be the start of something beautiful, and one little part of me remembered the motto of Miss Finch's School for Girls. Not the official motto, which was something boring like Faith, Integrity and Service, but the motto that the girls lived by—You Won't Get Caught.

I smiled at him. The rain spattered on me as I opened the car door. It didn't matter. I couldn't possibly have gotten any wetter. "I probably won't be any good," I said modestly, "but I guess it won't hurt to give it a try."

Four

By the time Tom came to pick me up to take me to the tryouts, I was looking forward to getting out of the house. Mother was playing the housewife with such enthusiasm that it was beginning to get on my nerves.

"I'll get the door," she sang when she heard the bell. She sailed off to answer it dressed in a frilled taffeta apron and carrying a wooden spoon.

"You must be Tom," she said when she opened the door. "How kind of you to give Susy a ride to the poetry reading."

"We'd better be going," I said hastily, grabbing my coat. "Don't worry, Mom. We won't be late getting in."

"Have a good time!" she called, standing in the doorway her wooden spoon aloft.

When we got to the car, Tom shot me a curious glance. "How did your mother get the idea we were going to a poetry reading?"

I squirmed. "Can you keep a secret?" I said.

"Yes," he said, looking at me. "I can keep a secret."

"My mother is an actress."

"I thought there was something about her..." he said, his eyes narrowing, "something familiar."

"She's known professionally as Maud Weatherly. She doesn't use her married name onstage."

He grinned suddenly. "Mr. Hardy is going to go out of his mind. Professional theater people right here in Hendleyville. And Maud Weatherly yet! She's his idol. He's still talking about seeing her in New York last year in that Noel Coward revival. I can't believe Rich never mentioned this. I can't wait to see Mr. Hardy's face. Wait till he finds out."

"He's not going to find out," I said. "It's a secret."

"Why should it be a secret? I don't get it."

"It wouldn't matter except for me trying out for the play," I explained. "But if I'm going to be in that play, I just can't face people comparing me to Mother. I don't even want *Mother* comparing me to Mother. That's why I told her we were going to a poetry reading. I guess that probably doesn't make sense to you."

"Oh, I understand, all right," he said.

"You do?" I said, surprised.

"I do." He grinned. "My grandfather is a minister. I don't like people comparing me to him, either. You can count on me. I won't say anything."

He pulled the car into a parking place at the side of the school. Several cars were already there. "Are you getting nervous?" Tom asked me.

"Not particularly. I guess it's the blood of all those performers pulsing in my veins," I said. "My grandfather was a song-and-dance man on the London streets and my great-grandmother was in pantomimes."

"I wish you could transfuse some of that blood into my veins," said Tom. "I feel like I'm about to pass out."

When we got to the room where the auditions were being held, Mr. Hardy, a short, balding man with a pointy nose, was handing out copies of the script for people to look over. I didn't need to look it over. I practically knew the whole thing by heart already. I wanted that part.

The audition room must have been used for something like chorus or orchestra practice because there was a piano and tiers of seats. A cluster of boys sat together near the door, and a larger assortment of girls were seated in twos and threes scattered over the room. They looked at us curiously as we came in.

"Mr. Hardy," said Tom. "This is Susan Howard. She's new at school."

"We're always delighted to have new members in the Players Club," Mr. Hardy said. "Have you ever done any acting, Susan?"

"No," I said.

"Just as well," he said, "No bad habits to unlearn, right?"

Tom shot me a brief amused look, and I realized with a sinking heart that now that he knew about Mother, he was expecting me to floor them all with my reading. It was the fear of this very sort of thing that had kept me away from the stage all my life. I hoped I wasn't going to have serious and lasting regrets about getting myself into all this.

"Perhaps we'll begin by reading Tony's part," Mr. Hardy said, looking over his glasses at the clump of boys sitting together.

For the first time, I realized it was very possible that one of the other boys would get to play Tony. I hadn't really considered that possibility before now, and I didn't like to think about it.

"Harris, let's start with you," said Mr. Hardy.

"Page sixty-four," urged Mr. Hardy. "Just begin at the top."

Unfortunately, Harris, a short boy with a broad, merry face, did a pretty good job of reading his scene.

Mr. Hardy beamed at him as he sat down and asked if anybody else wanted to read for Tony. "It's good experience to audition," he intoned, polishing his glasses, "even if you don't expect to get the part. Come now, let's not be fainthearted. We're all friends here."

Tom stood up. Mr. Hardy looked startled. "Tom?" he said.

"You wanted people to read for Tony," Tom reminded him, walking over to the piano.

"Yes, yes," said Mr. Hardy. "Splendid. Give it a whirl."

Tom took his place at the piano, looked at Mr. Hardy and paled a little.

Don't look at him! I thought. He doesn't think you can do it. Look at me. I let my pocketbook and script slip to the floor so the noise would attract Tom's attention. When he glanced over at me, I flashed him an encouraging smile, and to my relief, he didn't look at Mr. Hardy again but gripped the script in both hands and faced me while he read, "'I hope you don't expect me to be noble on an empty stomach. It's not fair. You always were inconsiderate, Louisa.'"

My heart leaped when I noticed that his voice got lower and he began to take on a rakish, slightly arrogant look as he read the part. I knew he had it in him. He was a much better playboy than Harris.

When he finished, he glanced anxiously over at Mr. Hardy.

"Would you mind reading just a little bit more, Tom?" Mr. Hardy said. "Try it from the top of page ten."

Harris began to look sea green as he saw the part slipping from his fingers.

Tom read on until Mr. Hardy held up his hand. "Do you think you can handle a part as big as this?" Mr. Hardy asked. "Wouldn't you rather cut your teeth on a smaller, less demanding role?"

"I want this part, Mr. Hardy," Tom said.

"I think you can handle it," said Mr. Hardy. "Mind you, it's going to be a lot of work."

Tom grinned and came to sit beside me. I noticed his hands were not altogether steady, but it didn't matter now.

"Now, who would like to begin the reading for Lousia?" said Mr. Hardy. "Angela? How about you?"

Angela darted a sharp glance at me before she took her script and stepped up to the open area near the piano. I had a feeling that she didn't like it that Tom had sat down next to me.

She was a small, well-rounded girl with dark curls, not at all bad-looking, if you like the type.

I smiled on her benevolently when she began to read. She was terrible. Absolutely terrible. Not only were her vowels flat as pancakes, but she put into the lines all the emotion and charm of a person reading a grocery list.

To my relief, the girls who followed her were just as bad. I began to feel confident. Unless one of these girls was Mr. Hardy's niece, I had the part of Louisa sewed up.

Mr. Hardy looked at me over his glasses. "Uh, were you going to read for Louisa?" he asked me. He had obviously already forgotten my name.

"If I may," I said. I moved over to the piano, laid the script on top of it and raised my chin. "'I haven't had just one life, Tony,'" I said thrillingly, "'I've had many. Splendid lives, all of them!'" I thought I was doing a good job with Mother's accent, which is sort of part British and part American, as if she had grown up on an island midway between the two countries.

When I finished, I turned toward Mr. Hardy in time to catch him with his mouth open.

"My goodness," said Mr. Hardy, pushing his glasses back up on his nose. "Did you say you had never done any acting? Well, I think we've found our Louisa." He looked down at the script and murmured, "Extraordinary reading."

When he looked up again, he seemed to be vaguely aware of the miasma of hostility emanating from the

other girls who had read for the part and added
hastily, "I'm sure we don't envy our Louisa the job,
do we, people? A very demanding role, indeed. And
of course there are many other roles that will be
equally rewarding. As we always say, there are no
small roles, only small actors."

Everyone greeted this notion with the silent con-
tempt it deserved. It was easy for me to understand
why they were annoyed. I was a complete unknown
who had come out of the blue to clobber them. But
I didn't care what they thought. I was Louisa, and
Tom was Tony and for weeks the two of us would be
playing love scenes together.

When the last minor part had been assigned, Tom
and I left quickly and made for home. I slid in the car
beside Tom and slammed my door closed.

"You were great, Susy. I knew you were the perfect Louisa. Didn't I tell you?"

"You were pretty good yourself," I said.

"I really wanted that part," he said. He started up
the car and pulled out of the parking lot.

I waited expectantly for him to tell me why the part
was so important to him. As we drove past a street-
light, the weird blue-white light shone in bars briefly
across his face and I saw that he was looking very
serious.

Finally I said, "Is there some special reason you
decided to shoot for being the star of the show?"

He hesitated. "Well," he said, "did you see how surprised everybody was that I could do Tony?"

"I guess nobody realized you were interested in the acting end."

"That's not it. They just can't picture me as a playboy, that's all. To them I'm a member of student council and honor court. Good old reliable Tom. They've got me pigeonholed."

"So you're tired of being popular and respected?"

"You're making me sound pretty dumb," he said.

"Well, no, I know how people hate to be typecast."

"I tell you it does something strange to your morale when people act like you were born a goody-goody."

"Maybe you should get into some trouble," I suggested helpfully.

"If you're going to tell me I should hide somebody in my room like that crazy girlfriend of yours, you can forget it," said Tom. "I live with my grandfather, and it would kill him if I did anything like that."

"Well, anyway, now that you're playing Tony, people will see that you're capable of being as irresponsible and unreliable as the best of them."

"We can hope. Want a ride to school tomorrow?"

"I don't want to impose," I said, trying not to glow too obviously.

"It's right on my way. No trouble. Pick you up tomorrow."

Dad's car wasn't in when Tom dropped me off at the house, so I figured he was still tied up with the endless committee meetings necessary to get the theater going again. Mother, however, was lying in wait for me. She was going over the bookshelves with a feather duster, a bit of stage business that fooled no one.

"Oh, Susy," she said with an air of surprise. "You're back! Why don't I fix us a nice cup of cocoa?"

Mother was showing all the signs of wanting a cozy chat, and I wasn't sure I was up to it after the strain of the audition, but I followed her into the kitchen.

"I didn't realize you were so interested in poetry, my pet," said Mother, busying herself with the cocoa.

"Oh, yes. Fascinated," I said.

"Isn't this something new for you?"

"I'm growing as a person. New horizons and all that."

"This boy Tom seems very nice," she said.

"Clean fingernails, honor court, student council, very reliable."

"Somehow he looks older than you," said Mother.

"Just a year or so older. He's a friend of Richard's. They knew each other at camp. I think Rich asked him to keep an eye on me."

"Oh, a friend of Richard's! How sweet," she said with a sigh of relief. "You know, sweetheart, it's so lovely that we can have this quiet time together in the evening, just the two of us. I wish I had been able to spend this sort of time with Cecily when she was growing up. Of course, I had to work very hard to give her the advantages I wanted her to have, and my work often took me away. I try not to blame myself too much, but I sometimes wonder if Cecily knew that my love was with her, even though we had to be apart. I'm afraid it hasn't been easy for Cecily, being the daughter of someone well-known. She has talent—you know how well she paints—but somehow the self-confidence just isn't there. She feels, I think, a little overshadowed. I've tried so hard...." She sighed and patted my hand. "Never mind, darling, you and I won't lose each other, will we?"

I was beginning to count the days until Mother's rehearsals started. I couldn't take very much more of Mother's hovering over me like this. It wasn't like her. Also, it was driving me crazy.

Tom picked me up for school the next morning. When we pulled into a place in the school parking lot, a girl in a red-and-yellow wool poncho, jeans and red boots got out a car near us. "Hey, Tom," she called. "Ready for that chemistry test?"

"I hope so," he said.

Her eyes widened when I emerged from the passenger side.

"Findlay, have you met Susan?" asked Tom.

"Hey, Susan," she said, flashing me a broad smile. "I'm Findlay Lamb."

Looking at Findlay's poncho, I began to feel my Reeboks and jeans were a bit understated. "Hullo," I said.

"Susan's just got the starring role in the new Players' production," said Tom. "She's going to knock 'em dead."

"I hope I'll be able to handle the part," I said modestly.

"Don't you just love the way she talks!" squealed Findlay. "Say, I guess you're not from around here, are you?"

A tall blond boy appeared behind Findlay and put his hand on her shoulder. "Who's the beautiful lady, Tom?"

"Susan Howard, this is Don Parker, the class clown," said Tom.

"Slander!" said Don. "I'll sue. Get me my lawyer."

A bunch of kids seemed to converge on us as we headed toward the school buildings. I eventually lost

all track of names. It was confusing to meet so many
people all at once.

I dropped out of the crowd at my homeroom, and
they surged on down the hall. "Catch you after
school, Susy," said Tom. "Meet me out front."

I went on into homeroom and found my seat.
"Where do you know Tom Brannen from?" asked
the girl in the desk next to mine.

"Oh . . . uh . . . friend of my brother's," I said.

"I've always wanted a big brother," sighed the
girl, a bright-eyed brunette. "I'm Andy Kaufman. I
don't guess you've noticed, but we're in the same
biology class. Don't you think biology is an absolute menace? I refuse to dissect a cat. Frogs were bad
enough, but I draw the line at cats. I'm going to get
my doctor to write me an excuse. Allergic to formal-
dehyde."

"I'm going to volunteer to take the notes," said
the girl behind me. "I never dissect anything. I just
volunteer to be secretary and write it all down."

I perceived that some invisible shell of ice had
broken when I had arrived in the company of Tom
and his friends. It appeared people were going to talk
to me, after all. Naturally, I would have preferred to
be a social success completely on my own, but I was
not in a position to be choosy. Every day I was reminded that I was in very foreign territory. I needed
all the help I could get, and I knew it.

Five

When I got home that day, Mother had a present waiting for me. I unwrapped the prettily wrapped package and discovered three books—the collected works of Wallace Stevens, a thin volume of verse by Elizabeth Barrett Browning, and an even thinner one by Eldred Whiffle. Each had been inscribed "To my darling daughter," so they couldn't even be returned or traded in for something I wanted. I looked up to see Mother's radiant face. "Do you like them?" she asked.

"I'm speechless," I said. "Mother, who is Eldred Whiffle?"

"Don't you remember, dearest, that divine little man who wrote a sonnet to me? He was at a couple of our parties. I think he was a cousin of Arnie's or something. I don't know much about poetry, I must confess, but now that you have this interest, we can read and grow together. Perhaps we can have poetry readings as a family by the fire at night. Doesn't that sound delightful?"

"Cookies!" Maisie called from the kitchen. "Come and get 'em, Susy."

I was happy to escape any further discussion of poetry with Mother. When I went in the kitchen, Maisie was already pouring a glass of milk for me. I began to drink it immediately. I needed my strength. I had always thought it was tough on Pinnochio that his nose started to grow when he told a lie, but even Pinnochio hadn't been forced to read the poems of Eldred Whiffle. It was certainly bad luck that just when I had decided to keep a few secrets from Mother she should suddenly be keen to share in every detail of my life.

"I hear you got a ride with Tommy Brannen last night," said Maisie, loosening a few cookies from the sheet with a spatula.

I drank more milk, playing for time. Whatever had happened to privacy around this house?

"He picked you up for school this morning, too, didn't he?" said Maisie, looking at me with her bright brown eyes. "Well, he's a really nice boy.

Really clean, too. Cynthia says he doesn't even get his shirt collars dirty, he's so clean."

"Maisie, who is Cynthia?" I asked plaintively. "And what does she have to do with Tom's shirt collars?"

"Cynthia's my sister, girl. You've heard me talk about her before. She's the Brannens' housekeeper. She's been with them fifteen years, ever since before old Mrs. Brannen died."

"Mrs. Brannen? You mean Tom's mother?"

"Tommy's grandmother, Reverend Brannen's wife. Tommy's been living with his grandparents since he was a little thing. And isn't he his grandfather's pride and joy! Honor court, student council, president of the youth group at the church—he's a fine boy, all right."

I began to sympathize with Tom's point of view. I could see how it would get to be stifling to live the only life you had as a good example.

"What happened to Tom's parents? Are they dead?"

"I'm not sure about that. I have to find out." She chuckled. "I forgot what it was like to live in a little town where people gossip about each other all the time."

I heard the phone ring, and a few moments later Mother wafted gracefully into the kitchen. "Just Susy and me for supper again tonight, Maisie. Mr. Howard has been held up at the theater again."

"More committee meetings?" I said.

"No, dear, I am thankful to say your father has *vanquished* those ridiculous committees. He's meeting with the contractor tonight about some unforeseen problems in the revamping of the stage. A *great* deal needs to be done to make the stage workable."

Mother restlessly turned to rearranging the potted plants on the kitchen windowsill. She was showing all signs of an actress who needed to start working on a part—unfocused energy, restlessness and a tendency to drive those around her crazy.

"When do rehearsals start?" I asked.

"Not for two months, at least," she said. "Which *seems* like a long time, but it really isn't, dearest, because once rehearsals start you and I won't get to see as much of each other and we must simply *seize* these moments and enjoy them!"

It was amazing how she drew all eyes to her, no matter what she was doing. Even Maisie and I, who were so used to her, had stopped to watch her as she exchanged the short geranium for the tall one so the arrangement was more symmetrical.

I rested my chin on my hand and looked at her thoughtfully. "Mother, are there any little tricks a person can use to give themselves stage presence?"

She gave one of her golden little laughs. "What a curious question, dear. Actually, Vera told me that she always imagines that she's holding a large red balloon when she goes on. And Leslie Banks once told me that she always pretends she's riding a pink elephant, so I suppose there are tricks of the mind like that, to make oneself seem more consequential. The idea seems to be to make oneself feel very important, very much worth watching.''

"Do you do anything like that?"

"I don't think so. Oh, if I were feeling very low, the way I sometimes did when Cecily was a baby, I might say to myself, these people have come to see *you*, Maud. Make it worth their while! Something like that.''

It occurred to me that Mother was probably born with stage presence.

"I have to confess," she said, "that I am the teeniest bit competitive. I don't mean that I'm a scene stealer, I just mean that there's no question that I will hold my own against anyone else that's on the stage with me. From somewhere or other I dredge up the energy to *shine*.'' Mother beamed at me. "Isn't it wonderful having the time to have a cozy little chat like this?''

I smiled and nodded. At the same time I was taking careful note of the tilt of her head and the way she had of looking warmly and directly into your eyes. I could use that in the play.

I had been spending a lot of time studying *Falling Star*, and I thought I saw just how it should be played. It was pointless to approach it by analyzing Louisa's motivations. It was not that kind of play.

The trick was to be in tune with the comic rhythms of the play. Good timing was essential. And I thought I saw how Mother's mannerisms could be taken just a notch further, exaggerating them slightly so the character of Louisa would add to the light comedy and the artificial world of the play.

Mother went back to fiddling restlessly with the geraniums. I could sympathize. She couldn't know it, but I was anxious to get down to work myself.

The next day, I found out we would be having all our practices for the play during fifth period study hall. I was glad about that because I always felt awful about lying to Mother, and this way I wouldn't have to be making up excuses to cover up for any more evening rehearsals.

I was very keen to try Mother's tip of pretending that I was riding a pink elephant, but at the first practice, Mr. Hardy seemed to be mostly concerned about keeping us from bumping into one another on stage, and we didn't do anything with our roles at all. He made a lot of marks in chalk on the floor of the stage so we would know where to stand. At first we kept looking down at the floor to make sure we were in the right place, but after a couple of practices the chalk was all smudged and we just ignored it.

The plot of *Falling Star* is simple. Tony, an irresponsible playboy, has gotten engaged to Neely. A certain awkwardness develops when everyone gets together at Neely's father's estate in the country for the wedding, and Tony recognizes Louisa, Neely's mother, as the lost love of his youth. After lots of sparkling dialogue, Louisa and Tony run off together, leaving poor Neely in the lurch. Perversely, the audience sympathizes with Louisa, not Neely, throughout. This is mostly because Neely is such a jerk. In a piece of inspired casting, Neely was to be played by Angela.

Friday afternoon as Tom and I were driving home from school, I said impatiently, "I wonder when everybody is going to have learned their lines. We can't really practice properly as long as everybody's reading their part off the script."

"I've been working on it," he said, looking guilty. "And I think I've mostly got it through the first act, but Mr. Martin keeps giving us those chemistry tests and I really haven't had a lot of time."

"I didn't mean you," I said. "It's Angela. She hasn't learned the first line. You don't think she is doing it on purpose just to sabotage the play, do you?"

"Why would she do a thing like that? Not everybody is a quick study like you. Have a little patience, Susy."

I thought about the way Angela kept sticking her foot out in the aisle in the dim hope I would trip over it. Actually, so far she had no reason to be jealous of me and Tom. No matter how carefully I examined what Tom said on our rides to school, I saw absolutely no signs that he was interested in me as anything more than Richard's little sister. Angela, however, had no way of knowing that, which probably accounted for the nasty looks she was giving me. "Did it ever occur to you," I said, "that Angela might have a . . . uh . . . special feeling for you?"

"Good grief, no," he said, looking alarmed. "I mean, we do student council together and all that, that's all."

"I have the idea she really wanted the part of Louisa."

"Sure," he said. "It's a much better part."

"Also, I don't think she likes me much."

He grinned. "Jealous. Stands to reason."

I wondered if that statement could be classed as a compliment. If so, I should bronze it. It was the first I had gotten from Tom.

"Don't worry about it," he said. "Angela won't cut her own throat by fluffing the part, and if she did Jenny could step into the role."

He pulled up in front of my house. "Tell you what," he said. "Why don't we continue this discussion over dinner tonight? We could go to the White Horse Inn."

I had a little difficulty catching my breath for a minute there. Was he actually asking me out?

"Sounds lovely," I finally managed.

He grinned. "Great. I'll pick you up at seven."

I went in the house in a daze. There was no sign of Mom, but Maisie was in the kitchen slicing ham. "Cold cuts tonight, honey," she said. "No point in cooking a big meal. Your dad's tied up again and your mother's going to some special meeting of the Ladies' Aid Society."

I sat down. "I won't be in for dinner, either," I said casually. "Tom and I are going out to eat."

"Well, how about that!" she said, putting her hands on her hips and regarding me with satisfaction. "Ain't that nice?"

"Yes," I said. "Very nice."

Mother took the news about my going out to dinner with Tom very calmly. There were certainly advantages to falling for someone with a solid reputation as a goody-goody.

I, however, was not so calm. My first impulse when I was getting dressed that evening was to revert to the way I had dressed at Miss Finch's—plenty of makeup and a platinum rinse. I wanted sparks to fly. I wanted Tom to look soulfully into my eyes and tell me that he recognized how Fate had drawn us together that rainy day. At least, I might want that. I was not quite sure. Perhaps a simple meaningful squeeze of the hand would be enough at first.

Mother poked her head in my door. To my astonishment she was wearing a mousy gray felt hat with a small red feather in it. "Sweetheart, I'm so sorry I won't be here when Tom comes to pick you up, but

Maisie will stay until you leave in case you need anything. The Ladies' Aid Society is having a banquet,
and I need to rush off.''

''Is that a *hat* you're wearing?'' I said. It looked
rather like a felt cereal bowl turned upside down.

She stepped in and turned around so I could get
the full effect of the gray suit and the blouse with a
few modest ruffles at the neck. ''Yes. What do you
think? *Very* Ladies' Aid, hmm?''

''A little plain, isn't it?''

''My darling, it would be impossibly dowdy for
Maud Weatherly—'' she dimpled ''—but for Mrs.
Howard of the Ladies' Aid Society, it is *just* right.''

When I got dressed, I took Mother's example to
heart. I reminded myself that Tom had grown up in
a minister's household and might be expected to have
conservative tastes. So when he came to pick me up
I was a fresh-faced picture of demure sweetness in the
blue crepe dress Dad had got me for Great-Aunt
Prudence's funeral.

He barely glanced at me. It looked as if I were
going to have to wait for that meaningful squeeze of
the hand.

''There's really only one decent place to eat in
town,'' he said apologetically.

The White Horse Inn turned out to be a sprawling
Colonial-style restaurant with what looked like every
car in Hendleyville parked outside.

"We have reservations," Tom told the hostess. "Tom Brannen is the name."

The hostess looked at the reservation book and made a face.

"Is there some problem?" asked Tom.

"Oh, no," she said, giving us her professional smile. "But it will be a few minutes, I'm afraid, until we have a table free. We have quite a crush tonight. If you'll take a seat here by the fire, I'll have the waiter bring you some coffee or hot tea. It won't be very long."

We sat down in two wing chairs upholstered in chintz that were artfully placed before a roaring fire. Brass warming pans were hung on the wall.

"I hope you're not starving," said Tom. "Something tells me it may be a while."

A horde of middle-aged ladies surged out of a nearby doorway and milled around us, and I spotted a gray hat with a small red feather bobbing among the crowd. Suddenly, to my dismay, Mother appeared beside Tom. "Sweetheart," she exclaimed, "how lovely to see you!" She sank gracefully into one of the chintz wing chairs. "I hope you don't mind if I sit down a moment. Truthfully, my feet are killing me." She looked suspiciously down at her sensible shoes. "It's these low heels," she said.

"Tom, you remember my mother, don't you?"

"Susy tells me you're a friend of Richard's," said Mother, smiling brilliantly.

"We knew each other at Camp Winnehaukee," said Tom, "when Richard was a junior counselor and I was a counselor-in-training."

"Rich is such a dear," said Mother. "So solid. So reliable. He never causes one a moment's anxiety. I'm devoted to him."

I personally wished people would quit talking about Richard. I was trying to move my relationship with Tom onto a different, more romantic plane and all this talk about Richard was not helping me any. "I thought you were at the Ladies' Aid Society, Mother," I said pointedly.

"But my dear, I *am*. Or at least I shall be as soon as the staff gets the banqueting room cleared out and allows us ladies to take our seats." She lowered her voice. "They're perfectly lovely people, dear, but not exactly *jolly*."

I became conscious of someone behind me and looked up to see a tall elderly man looming over me. His bushy white eyebrows, thick white hair and stern, commanding expression seemed oddly familiar. Then I recalled who he reminded me of—Moses, as portrayed in my copy of *A Child's First Bible*.

"Tom, my boy," he boomed. "And this must be Susan."

Tom scrambled to his feet. "This is my grandfather, Susan. Granddad, Susan Howard and Mrs. Howard, Susan's mother. Would you care to sit down, sir?" Mr. Brannen lowered himself into the chintz chair as if it were a throne. It was easy for me to see why Tom was in awe of his grandfather. I had never met anyone who seemed so exactly like an Old Testament prophet. He was overpowering, with a massive head of thick white hair and piercing dark eyes. Two pale, thin young men who had followed him into the room stood like sentries behind his chair. I supposed they were prophets-in-training.

"I've just had the privilege," Tom's grandfather said sonorously, "of speaking at a most promising evangelical congress. How good it is to know that there are those prepared to carry the word of the Holy Spirit into this sadly troubled world." He shook his head mournfully. "These are terrible times. The decline in spirituality that we see around us must grieve all thoughtful men."

"I don't agree," said Mother, speaking crisply but with beautiful, pear-shaped vowels.

All eyes turned toward her. "In troubled times like these," she said, in her strong melodious voice, "people thirst for a quiet inner voice, a still center to sustain them."

With alarm, I recognized a line from *Margaret and God*. Mother's competitive spirit had been aroused by the pastor's ability to hold an audience. Tom's grandfather was impressive, but I had little doubt that in Mother he had met his match. I tried desperately to remember what the playwright's views on religion had been. I hoped they were not heretical.

Mother leaned forward with a graceful gesture. "Spirituality glows even next to the pagan temple of the marketplace," she said, "even in the midst of blind ambition, even in the company of despair because our deepest, truest self thirsts for it, thirsts for it all the more because the world around us seems barren."

Mother clearly had the prophets-in-training in the palm of her hand, and even Tom's grandfather looked impressed.

She smiled sweetly. "As I said when I preached at St. Clements in the Bowery, spiritual gifts are not always found where we in our blindness look for them but sometimes in humble or even corrupt surroundings. Can we forget the story of Christ dining with the tax collector?"

I was beginning to feel faint. Had my ears deceived me or did I hear her say she had *preached*? She was getting completely carried away. I was afraid Tom's grandfather would any minute ask to see her ministers' union card.

Mother looked over my head. "Oh, dear, I must be rejoining my group. I see they are going in to dinner now." She cast a radiant smile on all present, rose with a single elegant movement and sailed away to the Ladies' Aid Society banquet.

And not a moment too soon. I had sunk so low in my chintz chair that if I sank any lower I would be sliding to the floor.

I was disturbed to see that Tom's grandfather was looking at me thoughtfully. "Your mother is a gifted preacher, Susan. I have seldom seen someone who can hold an audience like that."

"Oh, she's well-known for holding an audience," I said weakly.

"Does she have any open dates on her calendar?" he asked.

"Sir?" I said, startled.

"I realize that she may be booked up," he said, "but if she is available, I have in mind some engagements where her gift is sorely needed."

"I'll have to ask her," I said in a faint voice.

Mr. Brannen rose to his feet, looking more than ever like someone out of the Old Testament when he drew himself up to his full height. "I'm so glad I had the chance to meet your mother, Susan," he said. "Few women have such charisma."

Luckily, I did not have to reply to that. He strode majestically away, his young attendants trotting to catch up.

"He thought your mother was one of the evangelists at the evangelism congress," said Tom.

"What will I do?"

He grinned. "Better tell him she doesn't have any dates free on her calendar."

The hostess appeared. "I have a table for you now," she said.

Too late, I thought. I've completely lost my appetite.

When the waitress had taken our order and left, I said, "I can really see why your grandfather intimidates you."

"Oh, I'm not afraid of him," said Tom. "I admit there were times he had me scared stiff when I was little. One time when I was about six, a missionary put his hand on my head and said in this deep voice, 'I trust this one will be dedicated to the Lord.' And grandfather said very seriously, 'If there is a call, he will be dedicated.' Well, you know that business of Abraham starting to sacrifice Isaac? I had the distinct feeling I was going to be next. I had nightmares for a week."

"And do you have the call?" I asked.

"Heck, no," said Tom.

I shook my head to clear it. Missionaries and evangelists were as foreign to me as members of some strange tribe in the rain forest. I ventured timidly, "Uh, do you believe all that stuff?" Then I could feel myself blushing. I sensed it had been a tactless question.

"I guess it depends. I believe in God, if that's what you mean. It's evangelism I'm so fed up with, and if you were around it as much as me, you'd feel the same way. Like with Tanya Martin whose dad is a pig farmer—she said she never gets away from the smell of it on her hands, her clothes. Not that I'm saying evangelism is like pig farming," he said, looking a little uncomfortable, "but sometimes I feel as if I'd like to go someplace where I never met another person spreading the Word of God."

"I guess it's kind of hard to get away from them, isn't it? I mean, they specialize in going to far-off out-of-the-way places. You'd no sooner get to Timbuktu than somebody would pop up out of the bushes and hand you a Bible."

"They do a lot of good work, don't get me wrong," he said hastily, "and you have to admire the dedication."

"Oh, yes."

"I guess everybody gets tired of what they hear about every day at home," he said. "Don't you get fed up with the theater?"

I gave that question serious consideration and had to admit that I didn't. "It's not quite the same thing," I said. Then I remembered Mother doing her imitation of an evangelist and added, "Of course, there *are* certain disadvantages to being in a theater family."

"I guess so," said Tom glumly. I could tell he didn't think they were much, compared to the disadvantages of growing up with evangelists running wild all over the house.

There was a long silence.

"Read any good books lately?" I asked. This had not turned out to be quite the lovely, romantic dinner I had hoped it would be.

Six

Mother!" I wailed when I got home. "How could you do that to me? Tom's grandfather thought you were an evangelist! He asked me if you had any free dates on your calendar!"

She brightened. "That's really quite a compliment, isn't it? I believe he's quite a good judge of preaching. You know, perhaps I could fit in a date or two before rehearsals begin."

"Mo-ther!"

"Why, what is it, Susy?" she said, looking puzzled. "Why are you turning so pink, dear? You haven't got overheated, have you?"

"Yes, I have got overheated. How could you tell Tom's grandfather that you had *preached*?"

"Well, I *have*, you know. St. Clements invited me to speak when *Margaret and God* was such a hit. I preached to a packed house, too," she said with some complacency.

"But you *misled* him. What could have possessed you to start talking about spiritual values like that? Why? I ask you. Why?" I had the uncomfortable feeling I was beginning to sound like my father, but I couldn't help it.

Mother bristled. "*Some* people like to make other people happy. *Some* people try to enter into their interests and speak their language because it's the gracious and kind thing to do. I had no intention of misleading Tom's grandfather, and I'll have you know I think a good deal about spiritual matters, Susan Alice Howard! I must say, I think the tone you are taking is very unbecoming."

I clasped my hand to my fevered brow and groaned. "You don't understand. I want to make a good impression on Tom's family. I *like* Tom. What kind of chance am I going to have with him if his grandfather finds out that my mother is an imposter?"

"I *do* understand, Susy-Q," she said, softening at once. "I'm very sorry that Tom's grandfather got the wrong impression. I'll tell you what. I'll just go to him and explain the whole thing. After all, it's just a simple misunderstanding."

I thought about what Tom had told me at dinner about his grandfather's dislike of worldly fripperies, his stern and unyielding attitude toward frivolity of any sort. Would I be better off if he found out Mother was an actress?

"I appreciate the offer," I sighed, "but maybe it's better just to let the whole thing die down naturally."

Mother patted me on the head. "You just lost your sense of proportion for a bit, sweetest, because you like Tom so much. Believe me, I understand perfectly. Now listen, I have a lovely surprise for you. Your father has promised to be in early tomorrow night, and we're going to have a marvelously cozy poetry reading!"

"Lovely," I said in a hollow voice.

However, the poetry reading was not fated to be. The next afternoon, Richard phoned from college. When I came into the living room, Mother was saying, "But, of course, Richard, we would be delighted to have your friend. When do you think you'll be arriving? Well, of course, we could have Tom to dinner. I think he's perfectly charming. I suppose you want him to meet your friend, too? Tell, me, darling, what's she like? Couldn't you give me a little clue?"

"Of course, I'm sure we'll love her, if you do. No, your father's not here, darling. He's continually tied up at the theater, and actually I'm on my way over there right now to offer my opinion about the new stage construction. Shall I have him call you when he gets in? I know he'd love to talk to you."

"Well, all right, if you're sure. We'll all have plenty of time to talk when you get here, as you say. We're just longing to see you, Richard. Love and kisses, dearest."

Mother hung up the phone. She had a strange look on her face. "Richard is bringing a girl home," she said.

"Great!" I said. "So we'll get to see what she's like!"

Mother turned swiftly and impaled me on a look. "Susan, you know about this girl?"

I realized that I had made a misstep. After all, I had pledged to Richard that I wouldn't say anything to Mother and Dad. But surely now that he was bringing the girl home, the promise didn't apply.

"I don't know much," I said. "You know Richard. He doesn't give much away."

"Sit down, dear," said Mother. "*Tell* me about her."

"There's nothing to tell," I said, squirming uncomfortably. "I only knew that he was seeing somebody and all he told me about her was that she was 'special.'"

Mother looked grave and sat down herself. "I'm afraid my nerves aren't what they were since Cecily brought home her...her fiancé. I just don't think your father could take another shock like that, sweetheart. Frankly, I'm not sure I could, either. Do you know, I haven't heard one word from Cecily since Christmas?"

I did not like to ask if Cec was continuing to cash her allowance check. I figured she must be or else Mother would have reported her as a missing person. I just gave Mother a reassuring pat on the shoulder.

"It's so ghastly," she said, a tear glistening in her eye. "I don't even know if she's married or not. But you know, dearest, as I keep going over and over that awful argument we had Christmas Day, I cannot see that I could have done or said anything any differently. Surely she can't have expected us to support Derrick. Even if we had *wanted* to, I believe it would be wrong not to insist that married people be quite independent from their families." She grasped my hand tightly. "You do see what I mean, don't you?"

"Good grief, Mother, the guy was awful. You don't have to explain to me. I expect Cec's just sulking, and I don't think she's crazy enough to marry Derrick, whatever she says."

Mother sat up straighter. "Yes, perhaps you're right. How could a daughter of mine... But you know, Cecily's father was not so marvelous, either, and I married him." She sighed. "Young people can be very foolish."

"Buck up, Mum," I said. "Let's not worry about it until we know we have some reason to."

She got up, drying her eyes. "You're so right, dearest. I must compose myself. I don't want your father to see me upset like this. But you know, though I wouldn't dream of mentioning it to your father, there are one or two things about what Richard said that disturb me. He called this friend of his a *woman* rather than a girl. Don't you think that's a little sinister? Tell me the truth."

"But maybe that's just the way they talk at college. Don't they have a dean of women and a dean of men?"

"I hope you're right. I do *so* much hope so. But the other thing is, when I asked him to give me a little clue about what she was like, he said, 'She's hard to describe.' And I promise you, Susy, there was something *odd* about his voice."

"Odd? How odd?"

"I think he's concealing something."

"He's always concealing something," I said. "Besides, what could he be hiding? He's bringing the girl home, after all."

"But perhaps there's something odd about her."

"What possibly could be odd about her?"

"I don't know, dearest. I can only guess. Perhaps she's an Eskimo or a practicing fire worshiper or something. Perhaps she has a criminal record. I know we should be broad-minded, but I truly do *not* think your father could stand it if she has a criminal record."

"Pull yourself together," I said. "This is Richard we're talking about!"

She brightened. "That's true. Richard is so *sound*. Never a moment's anxiety have we had about him. I expect you're right. My imagination must be over-strained after all this business with Cecily. I shall just put it out of my mind. Sufficient to the day is the evil thereof."

She left for the theater looking vulnerable, but very valiant and brave, like the little ship *Revenge* sailing into the midst of the Spanish Armada.

After she'd left, I sat down and stared at the phone, worrying myself sick. I had done a good job of reassuring Mother, I thought, but the problem was I wasn't sure I believed everything I had said. I knew that Mother had an incredible sense of the way people betray their thoughts by their tone of voice and their unconscious gestures. It was a part of her stock in trade as an actress. If she thought there was something odd about the way Richard was talking, I was afraid she was right and that something really was the matter. Could it be that he'd already gone and married this girl? I wondered what the legal age of wedlock was in North Carolina.

I was still staring at the phone when suddenly it rang. I picked it up at once. "Hello?"

"Susy? Has Maud left for the theater yet?"

"Richard!"

"Don't shout 'Richard' like that," he said sharply. "I don't want this phone call broadcast to the nation."

"You just missed her. Do you want me to give her a message?"

"No! I want to talk to you. Is Maisie there?"

"It's her afternoon off."

"Good. We can talk, then."

I looked around me nervously like a conspirator. "What's up?" I whispered. By then my pulse was pounding. "Rich, what *is* it? Tell me! Are you in some kind of trouble?"

"Calm down. I just want you to do me a favor. I need to get a message to Tom."

"Why can't you just call him?"

"I can't risk it. His house is full of extension phones. Anybody could pick up on them."

"Richard, *what* are you talking about?"

"It's kind of a long story, but did you know that Tom has a mother?"

"You mean his mother is still alive?"

"That's right. She wants to see him."

"Doesn't she know where he lives? Why doesn't she just come see him?"

"This is where it gets tricky. You know Tom's grandfather, don't you?"

"I've met him."

"Well, you get the picture. I mean he looks at you and you turn to stone, right?"

"Tom's not afraid of him."

'Well, Tom's mother is. And to top if off, he's been paying her an allowance for years and years on the condition that she stay strictly away. If he finds out she's been seeing Tom, he would probably cut off her allowance in a minute."

I began to feel very uneasy. "What's wrong with Tom's mother, Rich?"

"Nothing's wrong with her. She's a nice lady."

"This doesn't make sense to me."

"It's crazy, all right."

"But how do you happen to know Tom's mother?"

"Well, I was at a night spot with some of the guys and they were doing a spoof of all the little towns in North Carolina, you know, a comic number. And the comic says, 'And who's from Tarboro? And who's from Hendleyville,' and so forth."

"But you're not from Hendleyville."

"Not really, but the guys sort of raised my hand up, kidding me, you know, and the next thing I know a waiter brings a note to me saying that this lady wants to see me, and it turns out to be Tom's mother. She was trying to figure out a way to get in touch with him without the grandfather finding out, you see. So I offered to do what I could."

"Wait a minute, this girl you're bringing home is really Tom's mother?"

"That's right. I thought we could all have dinner at the house and she and Tom could get to see each other. She's afraid if they go out somewhere that Tom's grandfather will see them together."

"But, good grief, if Tom comes to dinner and finds his mother here, he's going to die of shock."

"That's where you come in. I want you to find out if Tom wants to see her. That's the big thing. And then you can let him know that she's coming to dinner next Friday night. That way it won't be such a shock. But don't tell Dad and Maud or they might scotch the whole thing. They might not like the idea of putting one over on Tom's grandfather."

"I just can't believe Tom's grandfather would be so mean as to keep his mother from seeing him. I mean, is all this cloak-and-dagger stuff really necessary?"

"Tom's mother thinks so. She's very skittish about the whole thing. She has a hard time making ends meet these days, and she's really worried about that allowance."

I thought about it a minute. "Okay," I agreed finally. "I'll talk to Tom."

"Good enough, Susy-Q. I knew I could count on you. Look, I've got to go. I've just about used up my stack of quarters. See you next weekend."

After he'd hung up, I spent a lot of time trying to figure out tactful ways of telling Tom about his mother.

I considered several possibilities.

1. "By the way, Tom, I understand you have a mother..."

2. "Good morning, Tom, just wanted to let you know that your long-lost mother will be at our place next Friday."

3. "I heard from Rich the other night, and he happened to mention..."

Or perhaps the ever popular 4. "Maybe you'd better sit down..."

The trouble was, there wasn't any easy and natural way to bring up a subject like that.

Monday morning, when Tom came to pick me up, I got in the car feeling very edgy. "Are you okay?" said Tom, looking at me curiously.

"I got kind of a surprise the other night," I said. "I heard from Richard, and he said he happened to bump into your mother and that she really wanted to see you."

Tom didn't say a word, but it seemed to me that his face stiffened. Finally he said, "Where did Rich see her?"

"I think in Durham or something. But, anyway, if you want to see her, Richard was thinking he'd bring her home this weekend, and we could all have dinner together at our house."

"Is that why your mother asked me over to dinner?"

"She doesn't know about your mother. All she knows is that Richard is bringing home a friend from school that he wants you to meet."

"Did my mother happen to mention why she's just now so interested in seeing me?"

"Gee, I don't know anything about it. I'm just a messenger. Rich didn't think he could call at your house. Your mother is really afraid of your grandfather finding out that she's trying to get in touch with you."

Tom frowned. I was startled to see that when he frowned like that he had more than a passing resemblance to his grandfather.

"But if you don't want to see her," I said quickly, "that's fine. I'll just call Rich and cancel, no big deal. That's why he wanted me to sound you out, that's all."

He cast a warm look in my direction. "Not much fun for you, Susy. Sorry. It's just kind of a shock. Yeah, I want to see her. Why not?"

When we arrived at school, I felt as if I had run the four-minute mile. I am not at my best in the midst of family drama. I prefer to be taking a nice walk when really sticky things are going on like Oedipus finding out he accidentally murdered his father, or Medea deciding to toast all her kids and serve them up for dinner. And this had the flavor of that sort of thing. Give me a nice drawing room comedy anytime.

Richard breezed in late Friday afternoon with Tom's mother and her baggage in tow. I regarded them with horror as they proceeded up our walk. Tom's mother looked exactly like a stripper. She had very long, very black hair, part of which was wound around in a kind of doughnut on top of her head, and she was packed into a shiny green dress that was a size or two too small. When I opened the door to welcome them, I saw that she looked like a *middle-aged* stripper. Her skin had lost the dewy look of youth, and I suspected that the very black hair was dyed. I breathed a silent thanks that Dad had made me give up all that makeup and the hair rinse. I could see now that it wasn't at all the look I wanted.

Richard hugged me and then introduced me to Tom's mother. "Susy, this is Mrs. Brannen."

She smiled at me, showing perfect white teeth. "Please call me Azurée," she said. "That's my stage name. Nobody's called me Mrs. Brannen for years and years."

"Your stage name?" I said blankly.

"I'm an exotic dancer," she said with evident pride.

My one thought was that somebody should warn Mother. Obviously, someone should warn Tom, too, but I saw at once that there was no way to do that.

I had never admired Mother more than when she sailed in from the kitchen and caught sight of Azurée. There was a brief, telling hesitation in her step when her eyes fell on a woman who was clearly her own age instead of the dewy-eyed college girl she had been led to expect, and I saw that the color drained from her face, but there was no other sign of her distress. She held out both hands to our guest and smiled charmingly.

"You must be Tom's friend," she said. "We are so happy to meet you."

"Just call me Azurée," said Tom's mother, flushing with pleasure. "Everyone does. That's my professional name."

"Of course," said Mother. "And you must call me Maud. Let me show you to your room. I'm sure you'll want to freshen up some before dinner."

As Azurée followed Mom down the hall, I could hear her telling mother that she was an exotic dancer.

Richard gave me an affectionate pat. "You've been a brick, Susy," he said. "I knew I could count on you. Maud and Dad don't suspect anything, do they?"

"No, but..."

"Great," he said. "I'd hate for anything to go wrong at this point. Azurée was a mass of nerves all the way over here. Can you imagine? She hasn't seen Tom since he was two years old.''

"But, Rich—''

"Shh,'' he said. "Here comes Maud. I better get to my room. I don't want her asking me any questions.''

Mother and Richard passed in the hallway.

"Richard,'' said Mother beseechingly.

He pecked her on her forehead. "Great to see you, Maud. I think I'll change for supper. See you later.'' And he ducked into his room.

Mother walked toward me like a zombie. By the glazed look in her eye, I knew she was thinking of how Dad was going to react to the news that Richard was involved with a middle-aged exotic dancer.

She clutched my arm. "Susy...'' she said in a tortured voice.

I quickly pulled her into the kitchen, looking around to make sure we were alone, and sat her down in a chair. "Don't worry,'' I hissed. "She's *not* Richard's girlfriend.''

I was relieved to see some color flow back into her face. "Oh, Susy, bless you. You *know* something don't you, my precious? Tell me everything, everything.''

I had promised Richard I wouldn't tell Mother and Dad, but as soon as I saw Azurée, I knew I was going to have to, anyway. Who knew what kind of state

Dad's heart was in? This sort of thing could kill him. Mother wasn't looking too well herself.

"She's really Tom's mother. That's why Richard got you to ask Tom to dinner. You see, she hasn't seen Tom since he was little."

Mother was beginning to look more like herself. "It seems most peculiar to me, Susy. Why should Richard pretend that Tom's mother is his girl-friend?"

"Now he didn't say that she was his girlfriend."

"True, but he certainly implied . . ."

"He was afraid if you knew you might blow the whistle and tell Tom's grandfather."

Light dawned on Mother's face. "Oh, yes, the evangelist. Well, I must say I can see that he might be a little narrow-minded about this poor Azurée person."

"You see, Azurée is terrified of him and he pays her to keep away from Tom, so it's kind of awkward. But don't let Rich know I told you because I promised him I wouldn't."

She held my hand in both of hers. "Bless you, you sweet child. Of course I won't breathe a word, but we must get a message to your father."

Just then I heard the sound of Dad's tires on the gravel outside. Mother gave me a brief startled look, then jumped up and ran for the front door with long-legged strides. By the time I made it to the door my-self, she was walking toward the house with Dad, her arm around his shoulders, whispering very fast in his ear.

I breathed a sigh of relief. At least it looked as if Mother and Dad would get through supper without collapsing. Now all I had to worry about was Tom. I had the distinct feeling that the conversation at dinner was going to be a bit strained.

Seven

Dinner wouldn't be for another couple of hours, so I went upstairs to my room with the idea I would avoid any further wrenching scenes by taking a long bubble bath. I stood at my window and looked out, thinking how nice it would be to fly over the pine trees and away to some tropical island where bongo drums played all night and there were no awful family confrontations.

Suddenly, a pebble cracked against one of the windowpanes only an inch or two from my face. I jumped and stepped back at once from the window. A smaller pebble hit with a ping. Then I peered out the window and saw Tom step out from the pine tree woods and gesture to me to come out.

I could feel my heart pounding in my throat as I went downstairs and slipped out the French doors in the study. Anyone from the house could have seen me, and it might have been a little hard to explain why I was going to meet Tom. I thrust my hands in my pockets and tried to look as if I were taking a little walk.

I went across the terrace and through the garden, then sauntered as casually as I knew how into the wooded area, where pine needles sank spongily under my feet. Tom was waiting for me, sitting on a fallen tree.

"I saw Rich's car," he said. "They're here, aren't they?"

"They just got in," I said.

"Okay," he said. "Tell me the worst. What's she like?"

"Well, she has long black hair," I hedged, "and I think her eyes are light, maybe gray or hazel."

"She's pretty awful, huh?" he said glumly.

"Golly, I don't know what she's like. She just got here. Rich says she's nice."

He brightened. "He did?"

I decided I had better plunge right in and get over the worst. "You're probably wondering how she and Rich got together," I said.

"I hadn't even thought about that," he said. "The whole thing has been such a blow."

I took a deep breath. "Well, they met in a nightclub, I think." I explained how Tom's mother had found out Rich lived in Hendleyville and had approached him for help in getting in touch with Tom.

Tom immediately fastened on the crucial fact. "In a nightclub?" he said, his face filled with foreboding.

"She's an exotic dancer," I said.

"Dear sweet heaven!" he said softly. "You don't mean one of those people who take off all their clothes?"

"I think they use scarves, maybe, or costumes," I said. "I'm not quite sure. But as far as I know, it's honest work."

"Good grief," he said in disgust, "you'd think she'd be too old for that."

"Oh, I doubt if she's over forty. Gypsy Rose Lee went on longer than that. Uh, not that it's exactly the same thing..."

"It's the same thing, all right," he said grimly.

"Maybe she *is* getting a little old for it," I said. "Richard did say he thought she was having trouble making it financially. Maybe it's not so easy for her to find work these days."

"Don't try to make me feel sorry for her, Susy," he said. "It's a waste of time. This is a lady who dumped me when I was two years old and hasn't so much as sent me a birthday card since."

"It might not have been all her fault," I said. "Richard gave me the idea your grandfather has been paying her to stay out of the picture, and very likely she needs the money, you know."

He stiffened. "My grandfather wouldn't do a thing like that."

I didn't say anything. I was wondering why if Tom was so down on his mother he had ever said he wanted to see her in the first place. There was an awkward silence.

Finally, he said, "I don't know. Maybe he would do something like that. As a matter of fact, I can understand why he might want to. Is that her story?"

"I think that's what she told Rich. Golly," I said, "something just occurred to me. You know, it might be safer not to let Maisie know about your mother."

"Who's Maisie?"

"Our cook. She's worked for us for years. But the thing is, her sister, Cynthia, works for you. You know, I think it might be hard for them to keep from spilling the beans to your grandfather if they knew about it. But she's bound to cook and serve dinner tonight."

"Don't worry," he said with a wry smile. "She'll think my mother and I are strangers. We *are* strangers."

"It ought to be okay," I said, thinking it over. "It's not as if Maisie hangs around listening to what everybody is saying in the dining room. Usually, she puts the food on and you don't see her much again until she brings in dessert."

"This dinner is going to be a nightmare," he said.

I looked at him uneasily.

"Oh, don't worry. I said I would be there and I will."

"I think she's really counting on it," I said.

"Well, I've got to be getting home. I wish this were all over with." He took my hand. "Look, Susy, thanks. I knew I could count on you to sneak out here and fill me in. It's really a help to know what I'm up against."

He squeezed my hand and smiled at me, then disappeared into the woods. I had had my meaningful squeeze of the hand now. The only thing was, what did it mean? Was it a 'good old Susy, you're a brick' kind of squeeze, or was it something more than that?

After he left, I picked a few dry, wispy fronds of something or other so I could say I had been working on a dried flower arrangement if anybody asked. Then I tried to saunter casually back to the house.

Tom was quite late showing up for dinner, and at first I was afraid he wasn't coming at all, but finally I heard the doorbell and ran to meet him.

"Tom!" I said, relieved to see him at last. He was dressed in his best honor court-student council style, conservative and neat, but his gray eyes were dark with distress. "Come in!" I said.

Dad came down the stairs and advanced to greet Tom with just the right degree of manly detachment. "Good to see you, Tom," he said, shaking hands. I was relieved that Dad didn't look sympathetic. I was sure that was the last thing Tom needed.

Mother, Azurée and Richard were standing in an anxious-looking clump at the door to the living room, but before the tension could build any further, Maisie appeared with her hands on her hips and announced in no uncertain terms that the soufflé could not wait.

"Perhaps we'd better just sit down to eat, then," said Mother, leading the way to the dining room.

Tom pulled out my chair for me and took the seat next to mine, avoiding Mother's eye. It was obvious he had no intention of sitting next to Azurée. Mother lit the candelabra, and we had no sooner all got seated than Maisie made a determined entrance with the soufflé.

By candlelight, I noticed, Azurée looked rather pretty. It was odd to see that she had Tom's gray eyes and something of the same line around the chin, rather as if parts of her were a smudged carbon of parts of him. I wondered if he could see the resemblance.

"Do you like school, Tom?" she asked timidly.

"I like school fine," he said.

"College is more fun," said Richard, making an extra effort to relieve the tension. "If you like high school, you're going to be crazy about college."

"I hope that statement doesn't mean you're cutting classes, and going to wild parties, Richard," said Dad, helping himself to the soufflé.

"I was referring to the intellectual stimulation, of course," said Richard.

"Tom's father was in college for a while before he went in the army," offered Azurée. "I'll never forget the first time he came in the club, all dressed in his uniform, he was. I was so impressed, it was love at first sight." She sighed. "He was the perfect Southern gentleman. When he was killed in that car wreck, I cried my eyes out. I thought I was going to go crazy. But there... Time cures everything, they say, and now I just remember the good things. That's the best way."

I could see that Tom was torn between distaste and fascination. I guessed that there were a lot of things he would have liked to know, but he couldn't bring himself to ask her any questions.

"So difficult to be a widow," murmured Mother, passing the bread around.

"Yeah, it was awful," said Azurée. "I was all alone in the world with this little baby, and it was so hard to get anybody to keep him while I was working because I worked so late at night. Jim's mother said that was no way to bring up a little boy, traveling all over the country like a gypsy, and I had to see she was right. I had to think of Tommy's own good," she said, looking at Tom with damp eyes.

"So difficult to be a mother," murmured Mother. Even Mother's social skills were foundering in the soap opera atmosphere of the dinner table.

To everyone's relief, Maisie swept in with the entrée and side dishes, bringing us all a temporary respite.

Then Mother chimed in brightly, "I know you must be proud of Tom, Azurée. He does so well in school."

"His father was brainy, too," Azurée said. "I used to just love to listen to him talk. Just talk to me, Jim, I used to say. He knew every kind of thing, Shakespeare, the Bible, all that stuff. Of course, I knew he had had advantages I never had. I wanted little Tommy to have all that, too. Naturally, I wished I could of seen Tommy grow up, but Jim's parents never accepted me. I was just too different from them. They were always kind of hoity-toity, if you know what I mean. Thought Jim was too good for me."

I was alarmed to see Tom's pale face darken. I was afraid if Azurée started criticizing his grandparents, we might see some violence before dessert.

"Can I offer you more lamb?" said Mother, sensing trouble. "Let me freshen up your water. Lowell, do pass Azurée some butter."

Tom licked his lips. "After supper, perhaps I can drive you around Hendleyville, show you around," he said. "That way we won't have to bore the Howards with our personal reminiscences."

"Oh," she said, dismayed. "I didn't mean to bore you all." Her eyes filled with tears. "I'm so sorry."

"Goodness," said Dad heartily, "a charming lady like you could never bore me!"

"I think Tom's idea is simply wonderful," Mother chimed in. "I know you two would like some private time together to catch up on everything. Yes, that would be simply lovely."

"You must have seen a lot of the country," I put in desperately, "traveling around the way you do, Mrs. Brannen."

"Well, yes," she said. "I have been around some. I've seen some mighty interesting things. Every place has its own specialty. Like in Miami you can get a Mai Tai with fresh coconut juice, but in North Dakota you get the best hot toddies. Things like that."

"Very interesting," said Mother. "I don't think I've ever had a Mai Tai. Have you, Lowell?"

"No, no, I'll have to try one of those."

Everyone was relieved when dessert appeared. There was no lingering over coffee, either. Tom ushered his mother out to his car, and to our relief we soon saw their red taillights disappearing down the drive.

Dad gave Richard a deep look. "Planning to bring any more of your friends home, Richard?"

Richard blanched. Dad could always manage to reduce him to speechlessness.

Mother smiled charmingly at Richard. "Now, Lowell, you know that Richard was only trying to help the poor woman. It shows what a very sweet nature he has. I'm proud of the way you think of others, Rich."

"I just hope poor Tom lives through the night," said Dad. "He looked to me like he was sinking fast." Dad went upstairs with heavy footsteps. I think he was glad that this was one family crisis that wasn't ours.

"Dad's right," Richard said despondently. "Tom looked terrible. It looks as if I made a mistake letting Azurée talk me into bringing her here."

I was always surprised at the way Dad could knock out Richard's self-confidence with a single look. "Don't be silly," I said. "It's not your fault that Tom and his mother don't have anything in common. And Tom said he wanted to see her. What else could you have done?"

"What a mess," he said. "Have you ever thought how nice it would be if nobody had any parents at all? Suppose we were just hatched out of eggs wrapped up in hundred-dollar bills. Nicer, neater, no nasty scenes."

"But wouldn't we miss our families?"

"Well, I'd miss you, anyway, Susy-Q," he said, grinning.

It was several hours later, and I was thinking about getting dressed for bed, when I heard the doorbell ring and ran down to answer it.

When I threw open the door I was appalled to see that Tom had a white bandage on his forehead. My eyes flickered quickly to Azurée at his side and I saw her arm was in a sling.

"We've been at the emergency room," Tom explained wearily. "Car accident."

"It was awful," said Azurée, stepping inside out of the night air. "If Tom hadn't made me fasten my seat belt I might be dead right now."

A look flashed briefly in Tom's eyes that made me wonder if he regretted the precaution.

"It was a four-car collision," she said, impressed. "Think of it! There were all kinds of police cars and fire trucks and a newspaper reporter."

I thought I saw now why Tom looked so depressed. It had occurred to him, if not to Azurée, that being in a four-car collision was not the best way to remain inconspicuous.

"Did the newspaper reporter get your name?" I asked anxiously.

She flashed me a weak smile. "It's okay. I just gave him my stage name."

"Did you break your arm?" I said, eyeing the brown stretch bandage looped around it.

"Just dislocated it, that's all. But I feel pretty shaken up, to tell you the truth. I think I'm going to go right to bed. My knees feel all kind of weak and quivery." She smiled poignantly at Tom and then tottered off in the direction of her room. Mother and Dad were coming downstairs and she began repeating the story of the accident to them.

"Are you all right?" I said to Tom.

He touched the bandage on his forehead gingerly. "Just three stitches," he said. "I think I can comb my hair over it for the play."

I cast a glance over my shoulder and saw that Mother had her arm around Azurée and was walking her back toward her room. Dad came over to us. "Was there much damage to your car?" he asked.

"Well, if you look you can see it got banged up, but I can still drive it."

"You weren't charged, were you?" said Dad sharply.

I could tell he was thinking the same thing I was, that Tom shouldn't have been driving as upset as he had been.

"Nah, it wasn't me. Some idiot ran a stop sign, I think. Everybody started piling up, and I just couldn't stop in time to keep from hitting the guy in front of me. Well, I'd better get on home. My grandfather's going to start to worry, and I don't want anybody to call him up with news of the accident before I get there."

"Are you okay to drive?" said Dad. "You want me to have Richard give you a ride home?"

Tom smiled. "I'm fine. Oh, uh, I think Azurée is planning to go back to Durham tomorrow morning. You might just tell her I said goodbye."

I noticed he didn't call her his mother. "Good night!" I called, as he walked back toward his battered car. He turned briefly to wave, and I saw his teeth flash white in the dim light as he smiled.

I closed the door. "What a night!" I murmured.

"Don't worry, Susy," Dad said, smiling down at me. "Tom's tougher than he looks. He'll be okay."

"Well, anyway, it's all over now," I said with a sigh.

Eight

"Hand your scripts to me, people," said Mr. Hardy. "The time has come to do it on your own."

"But Mr. Hardy..."

"Can't we just have a few more days...?"

"You didn't give us any warning...."

The protests rose, but he was firm. "I will be the prompter," he announced, "but do not look at me. Look at your fellow players. Now get up there, people, and *act*. Remember to speak up—don't mumble."

I tried to hide my pleasure. At last we were getting down to the real business of acting.

Once we got going, Mr. Hardy had to do a good bit of prompting of Angela, but except for that, to my surprise, Act One went almost without a hitch.

"Very good," he said. "But Tom, I'm not sure we want to play Tony as Hamlet. Let's have a bit more carefree *joie de vivre* and a little less of the hidden torture look."

Tom swallowed. *"Joie de vivre,"* he repeated mechanically.

"You know, joy of living," Mr. Hardy translated patiently. "I see Tony as basically a thoughtless, giddy creature, one of life's butterflies, charming, attractive, but mostly interested in good times."

I could have told him that the problem was not that Tom didn't know what *joie de vivre* was but that he was having a little trouble getting the effect after a grueling weekend of traffic accidents and Azurée.

"You were hatched out of an egg," I told him under my breath. "An egg wrapped up in hundred-dollar bills."

Tom grinned.

"That's it," said Mr. Hardy. "Like that. Now once more from the top of Scene Three. Neely says, 'I'm prettier than her. I'm younger, too.' All right, Neely?"

"'I'm prettier than her. I'm younger, too,'" repeated Angela.

But you are a jerk, I thought, watching her.

" 'Must we keep talking about Louisa?' " said Tom. " 'It does not help me, darling, to maintain a proper romantic attitude when you keep talking about Louisa. Let's talk about our honeymoon instead. Do you still absolutely insist on Majorca?' "

" 'Majorca is so romantic. Oh, I'll be such a good wife to you, Tony. I'll be faithful and devoted and bring you your slippers and pipe. Mother could never be devoted like that.' "

" 'I thought we had agreed to stop talking about Louisa,' " he said sharply.

"Better, much better," said Mr. Hardy. "I think we've got Act One well under way, folks. Tomorrow Act Two. Now study your lines tonight!"

I folded up my script, feeling very cheerful. Act Two was when we got to the love scenes. I couldn't wait. As I stood up to leave, Mr. Hardy put his hand on my shoulder. "Susy," he said, "I just wanted to tell you how extremely pleased I am with your work. I don't like to make comparisons between students in class, but your Louisa has a polish that is well-nigh professional."

I blushed as furiously as if I had been caught stealing something. I suppose I felt I *had* stolen something.

"There's something about your interpretation," he went on dreamily, "like a young Maud Weatherly. I saw her, you know, in *Private Lives*. What a thrill! They don't make stars of that caliber any-more.''

I was glad Mother wasn't there to hear him talk-ing about her as if she were dead. It would have cur-dled her blood.

He gave me a brisk pat. "I believe in encouraging talent, Susy. Acting is a hard road, but I think you should develop that extraordinary gift of yours. I'll be happy to talk to your parents, if you like, about summer workshops in drama.''

"Thank you, Mr. Hardy." I gulped. "But I don't think I should let anything divert me from my planned career as a nuclear physicist.''

I scurried out as quickly as I could but I thought I heard him murmuring behind me, "Such talent. Nuclear physics! Such a waste!''

As we were driving home after school, Tom said, "I think the play's going pretty well, don't you?''

I blushed. "Mr. Hardy says I remind him of a young Maud Weatherly.''

Tom grinned. "No surprise there. Well, what do you expect? Your pedigree sticks out all over you. You're just plain better than the rest of us.''

"Oh, I don't think so," I said.

"Heck, it's obvious, Susy. You should be glad. If you're good, it's good for all of us, for the whole play. You should have seen what a disaster *A Mid-summer Night's Dream* was last year. But this year we've got a winner, something we can all be proud of." He grinned. "Even Angela is pretty strong when it comes to the part where Neely is acting jealous of Louisa."

"Yup. Angela is the perfect Neely, all right."

"And I don't think I'm such a bad Tony, either. I don't pretend to be professional caliber, but I think I'll be able to hold my end up."

"You're a *wonderful* Tony," I said.

"I have to work on that *joie de vivre* stuff. Not easy the way I'm feeling right now, with all that junk about Azurée. Believe me, I'm just glad I can talk to you about it. It's the only way I can let off any steam."

"Your grandfather still doesn't suspect that you saw her?"

"Nope," he said. "I'm afraid he might go up in smoke if he found out she came over, and yet, you know, she's not such a bad sort."

"Oh, no!" I said.

"I just can't understand why my father married her. No, that's not fair. Heck, she's sweet; she was probably awfully pretty seventeen years ago. I can imagine him falling for her. She's not so bad. But I don't think it's fair for her to come around making me feel obligated when she's never had anything to do with me all these years. Do you think I'm a creep for just wishing she'd go away?"

"Golly, no. Even the best mothers in the world take a lot of getting used to, and to have one sprung on you like that . . ."

"Let's face it, she is kind of tacky," he said flatly.

"Well, you live in different worlds," I said.

"That's it! We don't have anything to say to each other. We don't speak the same language. It's just kind of . . . painful. But she was talking about looking for work out West, so I guess I won't be hearing from her again, anyway."

"Especially since she's so afraid of your grandfather."

"True," he said, looking more cheerful. "I'm just going to try to put it behind me. It's interesting and all that, meeting her, but it doesn't have to throw me into a tailspin." He grinned at me. "I need to work on that *joie de vivre*."

The next day at practice, suddenly nothing would go right.

"No, no, Neely," said Mr. Hardy in exasperation. "You aren't *afraid* of Tony. You're a little insecure, maybe, but you're confident you can hold his affections."

Angela looked sulky.

"I don't understand it," he said. "You were doing it perfectly yesterday. Well, let's not beat it to death. Maybe you're just tired. Let's leave Act One for a while—" Mr. Hardy wiped his brow "—and move on to Act Two. Louisa and Tony on the terrace in the evening. By the way, Harris, how is that moon coming?"

"I'm still working on the wiring," said Harris.

"Better double wire it. We don't want it to fall on anybody's head," cautioned Mr. Hardy. "All right, folks, let's take it from the top. Tony says, 'Is that you, Neely?'"

"'Is that you, Neely?'" said Tom.

I gave one of Mother's soft, golden laughs. "'No, it's only Louisa.'"

"'Oh, Louisa,'" he said flatly.

"'I've always admired the moon, don't you remember?'" I said.

"'Ah, yes, it has a man in it.'"

"'Don't tease me, Tony.'" I put my hand on his chest.

Unfortunately, just as we were getting to that very interesting, delicate part of the scene where we have to convey that we are really very attracted to each other, I became conscious of a lot of whispering out front.

Tom turned a startled glance down to the seats.

"Quiet, please," said Mr. Hardy, striking a baton on the floor. "Start again, Susy, from 'Don't tease me, Tony.'"

Still the whispering kept up. "If I hear another sound out of you girls, Angela, Jenny," Mr. Hardy said wrathfully, "I'm going to pitch you out on your ears."

It was not the best atmosphere for working on a tender love scene.

I was beginning to get a little paranoid about those love scenes. Were we ever going to get them whipped into shape? Was this whispering a part of some plot of Angela's to see to it that we had to wing it on opening night?

After school as Tom and I walked toward the parking lot, I was still thinking about the bad rehearsal. I told myself I should try to take a professional attitude toward the play. There were bound to be ups and downs in any production. I should try to combat the feeling that I was doomed never to get in a proper love scene with Tom.

As we approached the lot, Don Parker caught sight of Tom and let out an Indian war whoop. "Leading a secret life, huh, Brannen?" he yelled.

Findlay, standing at Don's side, unexpectedly turned red and said, "Shh, Don. Be quiet."

Don gave us a broad wink. "Don't want Susy to start comparing notes with Azurée, huh?"

"What are you talking about?" said Tom, freezing at the sound of his mother's name.

I felt rather paralyzed myself. Where had Don heard about Azurée? What was he talking about?

Findlay kept tugging Don's shirt sleeve. "Cut it out, Findlay," he said crossly. "It's not any secret. Heck, it was in the paper."

"What was in the paper?" I heard myself saying.

"The story about the accident," said Don.

"Don Parker," said Findlay, "if you don't shut up and get into the car, I'm never going to speak to you again."

He got in the car, still muttering, "For pete's sake, it's not as if it's any secret."

After they'd driven off, Tom turned to me. "Do you get the paper?" he said.

"*The Banner*? Yes, we get it. I think we've probably got yesterday's copy still rolled up in the pantry."

"Why don't we stop by your house and take a look at it?" he said grimly.

When we got to my house, found the previous evening's paper and unrolled it, we learned the worst.

In the account of the four-car collision there was a telling paragraph that read, "Also treated for minor injuries were Thomas Brannen, 16, student, of Hendleyville, and the passenger in his car, Azurée, 25, exotic dancer, of Durham."

"For crying out loud," said Tom weakly. "She lied about her age."

"This certainly should help with your goody-goody image problem," I said.

"Very funny," he said coldly. "So now everybody in school thinks I've had some floozy up for the weekend and probably about a hundred and fifty of

my grandfather's parishioners will see it as their
public duty to call it to my grandfather's attention."

"Oh, dear."

It is possible that the whole thing would have
blown over quickly if it hadn't been that Tom had
such an impeccable reputation. If it had happened to
Don Parker it would have been just a good joke.
Since it was Tom, however, it wasn't so simple.

When Tom picked me up for school the next
morning his face was gray with fatigue.

"How'd it go with your grandfather?" I in-
quired.

"I had to tell him the truth. He was pretty upset,
but he understood that I might have wanted to see my
mother. The most awful part was the way the phone
kept ringing all evening. Granddad couldn't figure
out whether it would be better to claim the story was
a misprint or whether to claim I was trying to save
Azurée's soul. Finally, he decided it was safest to say
she was an old friend of the family, since that had at
least a germ of truth in it. I think he's spending today praying for forgiveness for perjuring his soul.
Oh, it's been bad, all right."

More fun was yet to come. Fifth period, Jenny
Marshall brought a note from her mother saying she
wanted Jenny excused from participating in the play
because of the dangerous atmosphere of moral turpitude at rehearsals. Mr. Hardy was flabbergasted.
Evidently, he did not read the local paper, either.

Mr. Smithers, the honor court's adviser, called Tom out of class for a conference and said it grieved him to have to suggest it, but he thought Tom had better resign from the honor court because of the public relations problems.

"What did you say?" I said, aghast, as Tom was telling me about it while we drove home from school.

"I wrote him out my resignation right then and there," said Tom. He gave a wry smile. "I cited 'personal reasons.'"

"But why didn't you just explain?"

"I just couldn't, Susy. I couldn't face it. When it came right down to it, I just couldn't tell him Azurée was my mother. For one thing, he probably would have laughed. It sounds like a pretty lame excuse, doesn't it? And then if I had been able to convince him I was telling him the truth he would have felt *sorry* for me! I can't tell you what a lowlife I felt like, standing there ashamed to admit that Azurée is my mother," he said. "All the time I guess I looked guilty enough to convince anybody that I keep a harem on the side, at least."

"It'll all blow over," I said.

"You don't know Hendleyville," Tom said glumly.

I grabbed his free hand and squeezed it. "It's not your fault, Tom Brannen, so don't you go kicking yourself about it. Not a bit of it's your fault. You just ended up in a mess, that's all."

"Look," he said. "Do you have to go straight home? Maybe we could go to the Big D and get some onion rings or something. The thing is, if I go home, that phone is still going to be ringing—loyal parishioners wanting to talk to Granddad. I tell you, I don't think I'm up to it."

"Okay. Mother and Maisie were going to the farmers' market this afternoon, so they won't be waiting for me."

He groaned as he turned the car in the direction of the Big D. "Moral turpitude! Good grief, what *is* moral turpitude?"

"I don't know," I said, "but it sounds awful, doesn't it? It sounds like some kind of disease."

We drove through the drive-in window and got a couple of orange drinks and an order of French-fried onion rings, which was the specialty of the house. Then we parked at the back of the parking lot facing some pine trees.

"I'll go crazy if I keep thinking about it," said Tom. "I keep imagining myself as a little old man leaning on a cane and people *still* whispering about the time I had a stripper up from Durham. I can hear the old biddies saying, 'Now stay away from old Tom, sugar lump. When he was sixteen he had a bad case of moral turpitude.'"

I grinned. "I know what my mother would say to that. She'd say, 'Dearest, it doesn't *do* to *dwell* on unpleasantness. I refuse to allow the petty minds of others to *poison* my life.' And actually, you know, she's got a point. She usually does."

His eyes crinkled with laughter. "I love to watch you doing a takeoff on your mother," he said. "That's what you're doing in the play, aren't you?"

"You noticed?" I said in a small voice.

"Sure, once you've met her and talked to her you can't miss it—the gestures, the way of turning her head. You're quite a mimic. I noticed it the day you were telling that story about your old school."

"My takeoff on Isabel *is* one of my better efforts. But doing a takeoff on my mother is a little riskier. She'd hate it if she caught me at it."

"But she won't. She doesn't even know about the play, right?"

"That's true," I said, brightening.

"I can see the temptation," he said. "She's perfect for Louisa."

"Actually, the character was based on her."

"You're kidding me?"

"That's right. Sterling Prentice, the playwright, was nuts about Mother. It broke his heart when she decided not to play Louisa."

"She didn't want it? But it'd be perfect for her."

"It might be *too* perfect for her. I've been doing some thinking about that lately. When she decided against the play, what she said was that she wasn't ready to start playing aging actresses. That made sense to me. You know, she really does not look her age. But since I've been practicing the role myself, I've started thinking there were probably other reasons she didn't like the part. In some ways, it's not a very flattering role."

"But Louisa's a charmer, Susy! Everybody's crazy about her. She *makes* the play."

"But she's a professional charmer," I said. "She's always on. A critic said that about Mother one time, that she was 'always on' and it really hurt her feelings. It wasn't quite fair, either. It's just that the theater is so much in her blood that it's second nature to her; the way she moves and talks is just bound to be a little theatrical."

"So she thought Louisa was a kind of caricature of her," he said.

"Yes, but I don't think that's the real reason she didn't like the part. I'll bet that business of Louisa stealing her daughter's fiancé was what she couldn't stomach."

"But it's not as if it's an unsympathetic part. Nobody cares about Neely. The whole audience is on Louisa's side. I don't see what you're getting at."

"Well, you know how I don't like to be compared to Mother?"

"I remember. You told me."

"I think Cecily, my sister, has the same problem. And Mother feels bad about it. She's such a . . . an attractive person, such a personality, she would really have to dim her lights if she weren't going to outshine Cecily and me. I mean she'd have to wear sackcloth and ashes and spend the rest of her life sorting potatoes or something or else we could *never* measure up to her. I mean, no matter how you cut it, we're bound to end up overshadowed by her because she's so special.''

He grinned. ''I think you hold your own, all right.''

''Well, I think she feels guilty. That's why she didn't want to play Louisa. It really is a nasty turn Louisa does to Neely, you know.''

''But in the play, who cares about Neely? Compared to Louisa, Neely is . . .''

''That's what I mean! Neely seems like such a creep mostly because she's completely outcharmed by Louisa.''

''Maybe you're right.''

''I'm pretty sure I'm right. You can see why it would be a double disaster if she saw me in the part. The thing is, I do sort of caricature Mother. But just because that's what the play needs. It's supposed to be a funny play. But believe me, if Mother saw it she wouldn't be laughing. Lately, I wake up sometimes in the middle of the night and realize I've been dreaming she's in the audience opening night.'' I shivered.

''Geez, families!'' he exclaimed in disgust. ''Why does everything have to be so complicated. Just think about it—if I didn't have to cope with all this business about Azurée and you didn't have to cope with your mother, we'd be sitting here eating onion rings and be as happy as the day is long.''

He threw our practically untouched onion rings into the nearest trash and turned the car back toward my house.

When I got in the house, the phone was already ringing. It was Andy Kaufman, my partner in biology lab. "Susy!" she said breathlessly. "Have you heard about Tom Brannen? He's eloped with a stripper. Can you believe it!''

"No," I said. "I don't believe it. I just saw him a second ago. We were eating onion rings at the Big D."

"You mean he hasn't eloped with a stripper?" she said.

"Sorry to disappoint you, Andy, but no, he hasn't."

"Well, I did hear some story that the police had picked him up when they raided an orgy, but I knew that was just a wild rumor. You wouldn't have believed how upset Angela was. She was stomping all over the gym sixth period and turning five different colors of red. I always thought she had some kind of a crush on Tom, but now she says she never could stand him and that she always suspected something like this would come out.''

"Angela is such a sweetie.''

"I know. I never could stand her, either. So what *is* the real story? I mean, everybody knows he had to resign from honor court."

"Very simple," I said. "Tom was just giving a ride to this friend of the family, and they had the bad luck to have an auto accident and that's how this whole thing got started."

There was a meaningful pause. Finally, Andy said, "I really do admire your loyalty, Susy. I really do. A lot of people think Yankees are cold and heartless, but you're not that way a bit. I think it's great the way you're standing by Tom through all his troubles."

"But, Andy!" I screeched, "he hasn't *done* anything."

"So loyal! So true!" she said, her voice quavering with emotion.

I didn't trust myself to say anything else. I just dropped the receiver back on the phone.

Nine

You have been irresponsible as long as I've known you, Tony Manners,' " I said.

" 'Dreadfully irresponsible,' " Tom assented.

" 'You'd make a frightful husband for Neely.' "

" 'Oh, frightful. You're quite right.' "

" 'I suppose I shall have to take you on myself, then.' "

" 'I'd say it's your duty.' "

We kissed.

I had waited for this kiss, plotted to achieve it, looked forward to it for weeks, but I had to admit it was not the thrill I had hoped. I was not sure whether this was because the kiss was written into the script, or because as it took place onstage we were being watched by the hostile eyes of Angela and her two girlfriends. They sat with folded arms on the front row hexing us with their eyes.

Mr. Hardy strode onto the stage. "Wonderful, wonderful. I feel very good about this play, people," he said, rubbing his hands together.

I shuffled my feet in embarrassment. The sophisticated poise I displayed when I played Louisa had a way of dissolving the second I ran out of lines to say. I was standing there feeling chilled at the thought that this was our final dress rehearsal. The next time Tom and I did this scene it would be in front of an auditorium full of parents, teachers and kids.

Mr. Hardy cast a critical look at my costume, a silver-colored dress with twenties-style fringe. He twitched its shoulder. "I think we need another half inch out at this seam," he said. "It doesn't seem to hang properly. Can you get your mother to take care of that?"

"Sure," I said.

So far, I had managed to keep *Falling Star* a complete secret from my family, but only with the kind of effort that made being a counterspy seem easy by comparison.

I had been smuggling my costumes home in a book bag and doing all the necessary alterations myself with a trusty needle and thread after everyone had gone to bed. The chief problem with this approach, apart from the way it left me short of sleep, was that it made it hard for me to bring home any books. I had skated through a couple of biology tests by the skin of my teeth.

"All right," said Mr. Hardy, raising his voice. "I want everybody here a half hour before curtain time. Does anyone have any problems with that?"

No one admitted to having any problems, and soon we were filing out of the auditorium.

"I have my cover story all set up for the night of the performance," I reported to Tom in a low voice. "I told my parents we were going to Durham to take in a movie, so we might be late getting in."

"Was that okay with them?"

"Well, naturally. They trust you completely."

"They obviously haven't heard the latest rumors," he said grimly.

"I think I better check the movie listings in case they ask me what we're going to see. It probably wouldn't hurt to read a few movie reviews, either," I said.

"Your folks don't suspect that you've been working on the play all this time?"

"Nope. They haven't a clue. I've been ultracareful. I even rehearse my lines with the shower going full force. Mother did sort of point out that bathing too often dries out your skin, but that's all. What about you? Are you still keeping it dark from your grandfather?"

"You bet. A couple of times I've almost broken down and told him, but he's been acting so weird since Azurée showed up that I think it's better not to risk it."

"Weird?"

"Jumpy."

I found it hard to imagine Tom's grandfather being jumpy. His making *other* people jumpy was, on the other hand, quite easy to imagine.

"If it weren't such a nutty idea," Tom went on, "I'd say he was afraid I was going to run away to live with Azurée. As if I'd want to run away with somebody who's a perfect stranger to me. Also, he goes around acting like he's afraid I'm going to turn out like her. What do you imagine he's thinking of? I mean, obviously I don't have any future as an exotic dancer."

"I don't know, but maybe this isn't the best time for him to see you playing a reckless playboy," I said.

"You can say that again. For that matter, I don't think it's the best time for the entire school to see me being a playboy."

"Are you still worrying about all the gossip?" I said. "I thought you wanted to kick your goody-goody image. So you've done it. Enjoy!"

"I don't like it as much as I thought I would. Jenny Marshall and Angela act like I've got something that's catching. But even that's not as bad as all the girls who giggle and sort of look at me out of the

corners of their eyes. On top of that, Don and Mike
are mad that I don't give them the real lowdown on
what happened. They don't seem to believe that
Azurée is an old friend of the family. Wonder why.
And all my ex-colleagues on the honor court are acting extra *nice* to me. I guess they feel sorry for me.
You're practically the only person in the school that's
treating me like a normal human being.''

I felt a little guilty. I had wanted to get to be close
to Tom, but I certainly hadn't wanted it to happen
this way. Closeness through social ostracism had not
been part of my plan. ''They need time to get used to
a new idea of you,'' I said. ''They had the idea you
were perfect.''

He groaned. ''You know, the funny thing is, with
everybody acting like you're some kind of criminal
or something, the next thing you know, you end up
feeling guilty. Sometimes I have to remind *myself*
that I haven't done anything. I can see now why these
weirdos go in confessing to crimes they haven't even
committed.''

I looked at him thoughtfully before I turned to go
into biology class. ''You know something? You're
letting all this stuff get to you too much. I'll bet
what's wrong is that underneath you've got a bad
case of opening night jitters.''

He smiled. Golly, he really was attractive, I
thought. I melted against the door to biology class as
he beamed the smile at me.

He restlessly pushed his hair back with his fingers. Since he had had to start combing it down on one side to cover the stitches, it seemed to bother him. "So you think I'll start feeling better after the play is over, huh?" he said.

"Yup. Don't you have this kind of sinking feeling in your stomach? Your hands and feet feel cold? You wish you were dead?"

"That about sums it up," he said.

"Stage fright, that's all," I said. "Tomorrow you'll feel like a different person."

"Hey," he said. "I've had it with being a different person. I want to go back to being good old stodgy Tom."

I grinned and gave him a playful shove.

"See you at lunch," he said.

Andy was waiting for me inside next to our lab table, looking at me with wide eyes. "Your parents don't care if you run around with Tom?" she said.

"No," I said shortly. I had given up trying to persuade Andy that Tom was an innocent victim of circumstances.

"They must be very broad-minded," she said. She pulled out her dissecting kit and added thoughtfully, "Of course, they're not from around here," as if that explained everything.

"Coming to the play tonight?" I said.

"You bet!" she said. "I hear you've got a real big part. Aren't you nervous?"

"Not very," I said, thrusting my cold hands in my pockets. They seemed to have started shaking a little.

That night after supper I carefully folded my silver dress and stashed it in my book bag with my makeup kit and a hand mirror. I couldn't very well leave the house with my stage makeup on—Louisa wore false eyelashes—so I was going to do my face at school. When I heard Tom's car crunching on the gravel of the drive, I hoisted my book bag and headed for the door.

"You're taking a book bag to the movies?" Dad said.

"Oh, well, you know, thought I might crack a book or two on the drive over," I said. Feeling that did not sound very convincing, I added, "I've gotten kind of behind in English."

"I see," said Dad.

Suddenly I noticed that Mother was all dressed up. She was wearing her burgundy Balmain, a heavy silk dress I have always admired for its clean lines and simple elegance. Ruby earrings glinted discreetly at her ears. I looked at her a moment in simple admiration before it occurred to me to wonder where she was going. Not to the Ladies' Aid Society, that was certain.

"Your father and I are going out this evening, too," she said. "To a community cultural event."

I was too taken up brooding about my upcoming performance to give much thought to Hendleyville's cultural events. "You look great," I said, smiling wanly.

"I hope I shall be worthy of the occasion," she said.

Tom rang the doorbell and I ran to the door, dragging my book bag behind me.

Tom blinked a little at the sight of Mother. She could have been a picture personifying glamour, standing there in the pool of light cast by Dad's reading lamp, her sable draped over a chair. But like me, all Tom was thinking about was the play. "Ready, Susy?" he said. "Uh, see you later, Mr. Howard, Mrs. Howard."

Once we got to the school and I started getting into Louisa's clothes and Louisa's makeup, I began to feel more calm. Mr. Hardy danced around us, lining everyone up and agitatedly reminding us of our cues. Angela peeked through the curtain and blanched. "Golly, there's a mob out there," she whispered.

Music began playing, and the sounds of shuffling and talking out front quieted.

"Scene one," Mr. Hardy whispered harshly. "Come on Angela. Now remember to *speak up*." He all but pushed her out on stage with Tom and the curtain began slowly going up. I heard Angela's flat voice saying, "'A full moon, Tony. Isn't that romantic!'"

"'Oh, quite,'" said Tom in a bored voice. "'Moon, June, soon, honeymoon, buffoon. I must confess, Neely, my love, that I find the moon just a shade hackneyed.'"

She giggled. "'Oh, Tony!'"

Soon Harris, with a carnation in his buttonhole to complete his costume as my stuffy ex-husband, Desmond, took my arm. A cold rush of fear washed over me as we stepped out on the stage, but just as suddenly it disappeared, leaving me in a kind of unearthly calm. I was pretending for all I was worth that I was riding on a pink elephant. I was also concentrating on being Louisa.

"'Why, yes, we've met,'" I drawled, extending a gloved hand. I fixed Tom with one of mother's long, intimate looks. "'Wasn't it in Bombay?'"

"'During the monsoon,'" said Tom.

"'So wet, the monsoon,'" I said. "'And you were on your way to Afghanistan.'"

"'Very dry, Afghanistan,'" he said, giving me a smoldering look.

I pirouetted away quickly, avoiding his eyes. "'You played polo in Poona,'" I said lightly. I was timing my dialogue by heartbeats as if I had my fingertips on the audience's pulse. I had a feeling of intense concentration and electric excitement as if I were a hunter stalking dangerous big game. Suddenly I realized now that *this* must have been what drew Mother to the stage and what had kept her there all these years, this excitement.

When I exited stage right after the first scene Mr. Hardy patted my shoulder and murmured, "Splendid," but I scarcely noticed. I spent intermission shivering in the dressing room, thinking about my discovery of the thrill of acting, while Mr. Hardy passed around soft drinks, slices of pizza and words of encouragement. "Splendid, splendid," he kept saying. "Now keep remembering to speak up. Harris, don't forget that we've moved the fountain behind the garden seat. We don't want you tripping over it." Mr. Hardy was obsessed by the idea that we were going to trip, stumble, bang into things or get clobbered by scenery. It made me wonder if he had suffered major traumas in summer stock or something.

And in no time we were back on stage. By Act Three I knew that I was in love with the audience. To hear its perfect silence as it hung on our words, to wring laughter from its throat was a thrill I knew I wanted to feel again and again.

It had hit me that acting was a game and that I was *good* at it. I knew that as positively as if the skies had opened up and some deep voice had boomed, "This one's an actress!"

As if Tom picked up on my excitement, I began to see an almost giddy playfulness in his performance.

No one would have recognized that underneath was the sober former member of the honor court.

"'Neely takes after her father,'" I said.

"'A worthy man,'" he said.

"'Oh, yes,'" I said.

"'I don't know how it is with me, but worthy persons always bore me. I daresay it's some fixation, don't you know. Probably scared by a parson in me pram.'"

"'You mustn't say that worthy persons are boring,'" I chided him. "'It's wicked. Saying what you think is always wicked.'"

The lines that had seemed a trifle flat after so much rehearsal seemed to come to life in front of the audience. Working with Tom was like playing a duet with instruments perfectly in tune. Talking contrapuntally, we inched our way toward the denouement.

"'You'd make a frightful husband for Neely.'"

"'Oh, frightful. You're quite right.'"

"'I suppose I shall have to take you on myself, then.'"

"'I'd say it's your duty.'"

We kissed and slowly the curtain fell.

Tom at once pulled out a handkerchief and wiped his brow. I grinned at him. "Fun, huh?"

"You've got a funny idea of fun," he said. The curtain went up again, and all at once the whole cast was holding hands and smiling into the dark auditorium for curtain call while applause welled up around us. This is it, I thought, the smell of greasepaint, the roar of the crowd, I love it, I love it. Then a movement caught my eye at the side exit, and I caught a glimpse of a sable coat and the glint of ruby earrings in the gloom under the red exit light.

I cast an agonized look at Tom who was standing next to me, smiling with all the *joie de vivre* in the world. When the applause began to die and the curtain fell, I ran offstage. Tom was fast after me. "Something wrong?" he panted.

"It's Mother," I said over my shoulder. "I think she's out there."

Mr. Hardy caught me as I ran offstage and handed me a long-stemmed carnation with a little speech of congratulation that I scarcely heard. He had a carnation for everyone. It was very sweet of him, really, but I didn't even remember to thank him. I just staggered back to the dressing room.

"What makes you think she was out there?" Tom said as I collapsed onto a folding chair in the bleak dressing room. I noticed that the paint was peeling off the plaster on the ceiling, leaving a bare spot the shape of a rabbit.

"I think I saw her."

"It's got to have been your imagination."

"Boys aren't allowed in the girls' dressing room," said Angela pointedly.

"Oh, buzz off, Angela," said Tom.

I swallowed hard. "You're right. It must have been my imagination. If she'd come, she would have come backstage, right?"

Just then the door to the dressing room was flung open and in swept Mother in her sable and rubies. "My pet!" she said. I noticed that tears were glistening in her eyes as she embraced me, but I didn't know whether that was a good sign or not.

Dad stood behind looking embarrassed. "A... uh...remarkable performance, Susy," he said. "And that's our unbiased view, isn't it, Maud?" He shook Tom's hand. "Very strong performance, Tom. I was impressed."

"You aren't mad at me?" I said to Mother.

She had a distant look in her eye I couldn't quite fathom. "My darling, I... well, I'm at a loss for words."

"Your mother means that she admires your artistry, while she deplores your sensibility," Dad said dryly. "To think that we have nourished this snake at our bosom all these years."

"Then you *are* mad?" I said, confused.

Mother hugged me again, getting my makeup all over her fur. "Of course we aren't angry, dearest. We're thrilled. Absolutely thrilled."

Just then Mr. Hardy opened the door and, seeing Mother, turned white and looked as if he were going to pass out. "M-Miss Weatherly," he said. "What an honor! Susy, why didn't you tell me?" he said.

"Mother, Dad, this is Mr. Hardy, my drama teacher," I said.

"I saw you in *Private Lives* last year," gushed Mr. Hardy. "An exquisite performance, if I may say so. My goodness, no wonder Susy was nonplussed when I said she reminded me of the young Maud Weatherly," he said, giving a merry laugh.

Mother winced. It had not escaped her attention that if I were "the *young* Maud Weatherly," then that made her the old one. But she rallied bravely and put her arms around my waist. "She's good, isn't she?" she said, giving me a fond look.

Just then Richard came in, escorting a pretty little blonde who kept stealing worshipful glances up at him.

"Rich!" I said, reaching out to him.

He strode over to me and kissed me on the forehead. "I didn't know you had it in you, Susy-Q, a brilliantly vicious performance. This is Millicent, about whom you've heard me speak."

I noticed that Millicent wore a single strand of pearls around her neck. What a relief it must have been to Mom and Dad to meet her. She couldn't have looked more harmless. "So happy to meet you," she whispered.

"I wonder if I might just have your autograph," said Angela's mother, inching up to Mother. "We have the album from *Chopsticks*. I just love it. Tell me, is Burton Denning as handsome as he looks on the cover?"

"Why, yes," said Mother, "I suppose he is." She smiled brilliantly as she scrawled her signature on Mrs. Benson's program.

Mrs. Benson wagged her finger at me. "Someday we'll be getting *your* autograph, young lady. All the young people did such a fine job, didn't they? My Angie's been practicing her lines until I could practically say them myself, but it all paid off tonight."

"Tom!" boomed a sonorous voice from the doorway. All chitchat immediately ceased. Tom's grandfather had that effect on people. He stood at the doorway of the dressing room looking like a prophet of doom.

Tom instinctively began scrubbing makeup off his face. "Good evening, sir. Did you catch the performance?"

"I did," said Tom's grandfather sternly. "No thanks to you."

Mother took in the situation with a glance and immediately threw out her arms and began sweeping us all out of the dressing room. "Mr. Brannen, you must bring Tom back to our house and we'll all have...a cup of nourishing cocoa or something. Really, I won't take no for an answer."

Tom's grandfather took in Mother's sable coat and her ruby earrings in a look of utter bewilderment, and I recalled that he had last seen her disguised as an evangelist.

As we left, Mother took Mr. Hardy's hand in both of hers. "Mr. Hardy," she began.

"Oh, do call me Oswald," he breathed.

"Oswald," she said with a warm smile, "I think your production was simply splendid, and you must come to brunch next Sun—" She suddenly remembered Tom's grandfather and changed course midstream. "I mean, tea next Saturday at four. Don't dress please, and we'll have a nice long chat about drama. I would be so interested to hear your views of Prentice's comedic approach."

As she swept out, bearing us all along in her wake, Rich winked at me.

Tom caught the look we were giving each other, took my hand and said, "Okay, but one thing you have to give your mother is she's a real class act."

I couldn't deny it. As we were walking out to Tom's car, I saw Don opening the car door for Findlay to get in. He waved at us. "Nice going, Tom," he called. "You all did a real good job." Findlay smiled broadly in our direction. I had the feeling that the thaw toward Tom was beginning.

Ten

Indeed I'm flattered that you took me for an evangelist," Mother was saying to Tom's grandfather when we got back to the house. She looked soulfully into his eyes. "I have always had a deep interest in spiritual matters. Perhaps if my life had been different..."

"Maud," said Dad brutally, "you'd better get to that hot chocolate you mentioned."

"What I don't understand," I said, as Mother disappeared into the kitchen, "is how you found out about the play. I was so careful to keep it a secret."

"Well," Dad said, ticking off his fingers, "1) Maisie's cousin, Elvira, who works at the school peeked in on Act One and reported that it was a stitch; 2) Angela's mother is our bank teller, and she told me three times that Angela just about had her lines down pat and kept asking me how you were coming along with yours; 3) My barber suggested that you were going to be a chip off the old block; and 4) The performance was advertised in the local paper with you and Tom listed as stars."

I thought of all the hours I had spent slaving with needle and thread to keep them from finding out, and they had known all along! Why hadn't I remembered what Maisie said about people in a small town talking about one another all the time?

Tom cleared his throat and turned toward his grandfather. "I would have mentioned it to you, sir, but knowing that you had a lot on your mind lately..."

"You don't have to explain why you didn't tell *us*, Susy," said Dad dryly. "It's quite plain."

Mother made an entrance with the hot chocolate in mugs on a tray.

"I believe we are celebrating the emergence of two fine talents tonight," Dad said, twinkling at me. "It's a pity we don't have any champagne."

I heard Mother whisper to him, "They don't ink-dray, darling."

"Spirituous liquors are never necessary for true celebration," intoned Tom's grandfather.

"Oh, no, indeed," said Mother brightly. "Would anyone care for marshmallows?"

"The play was a distressingly frivolous sort of entertainment," Tom's grandfather rumbled. "And I fear the writer was sadly lacking in moral principles. I cannot say I found it edifying to see people behaving in such a singularly irresponsible way." He looked at Tom as if holding him personally responsible for the play's shortcomings.

"I thought it was very well done," Rich said bravely. Millicent looked at him adoringly. It occurred to me that Millicent was just what he needed to give him self-confidence.

"It was well done," said Tom's grandfather ponderously.

Dad began, "Of course, the staging..."

But Tom's grandfather mowed him down mercilessly. "When I say well done," he went on, "I am not sure that is a compliment. To employ talent in such a frivolous cause is not to be commended, and the better done it is, perhaps the more reprehensible."

We all sat there looking at him in awe as if Moses had just returned to find us dancing around the golden calf.

"Oh, come on," said Tom, grinning at him. "We can all use a good laugh now and then."

I was sure that if Tom's grandfather had laughed I would have found the spectacle terrifying. However, to my surprise he did unbend enough to smile at Tom. It was plain that he adored Tom, which might have been why Tom was the only person who wasn't afraid of him.

"I suppose laughter can be useful," Mr. Brannen conceded in sonorous tones. "Still, I can't deny I found it disturbing to see you up there acting as if—"

"Tom did a lovely job with Tony," Mother said quickly. "So difficult to get that gaiety of heart that underlies the blasé facade. *Not* the easiest of roles, particularly for Tom, who is himself such a *very* different type."

"Tom was very convincing," said his grandfather. "In truth, I found it quite unsettling. I cannot deny that this sort of thing takes a certain degree of talent, but I would be very sorry to see Tom developing this talent. I could not in good conscience recommend acting as a career."

"That's precisely what I'm always saying myself," said Mother, smiling brilliantly. "But it doesn't seem to discourage anyone a bit."

"It's kind of early days to be thinking of careers," Tom pointed out. "First there's college. I think I'll probably want to develop an interest in accounting. That might not leave much time for amateur theatricals."

Tom's grandfather cheered noticeably at this. I realized that he had really been very shaken by the performance. Just then the phone rang, and Mother sped off to answer it.

"I think we should all be giving thanks," said Dad, knocking the bowl of his pipe against an ashtray, "that nobody got brained tonight by that plywood moon. It must have weighed ten pounds, and I saw one of the wires give way during Act One."

"I stood clear of it," said Tom, grinning. "I never did trust Harris's engineering skills."

Mother returned and, sweeping the skirt of her Balmain to the side with one hand, settled gracefully in her chair, looking a bit dazed. "That was Cecily," she said.

"Did she marry that creep?" I asked.

"It seems not," said Mother. "She was calling to ask for an advance on her allowance. She's dropping out of school to become a street mime."

"Probably be pretty good at it," Dad said dispassionately.

"I certainly didn't imagine, as I worked myself to the bone to send her to the finest schools in the kingdom," Mother said tearfully, "that she would end up a street mime!"

"But it runs in the family," I said. "Didn't you say that Grandfather used to be a busker?"

"Oh, cheer up, Maud," Dad said. "It won't last."

"That's true," said Mother, brightening slightly. "I believe you *never* hear of elderly street mimes."

"Well, Millicent and I had better be shoving off," said Rich. "We've got a drive ahead of us."

"We'd better be going, as well," said Tom's grandfather. "Thank you very much for the cocoa, Mrs. Howard." He got up and moved toward the door, looking at Tom expectantly.

Tom only sank more deeply into the couch cushions and put his arm around me. "You go on, Granddad. I'll be home later."

Tom's grandfather shot him a thunderous look, lowered eyebrows and all, but then thought better of it. "Well," he said, "harrumph. Don't make too late a night of it, Tom."

Rich and Millicent made their departure as soon as Mr. Brannen pulled his car out of the driveway. Then Dad announced he needed to read over a script and retired to the study.

"It looks as if it'll be just the three of us," Mother said, sipping her hot chocolate. But then, noticing Tom's arm around me, she suddenly rose from her chair. "I'd love to chat," she said. "But really, I suppose I had better be studying scripts myself. You know, I have never played Shakespeare before and I am just the teeniest bit edgy about it."

After she'd swept away upstairs, Tom murmured in my ear, "Alone at last."

"We can't go on meeting like this." I grinned.

"Weren't you surprised the way our families showed up like that?"

"Surprised? Appalled is more like it. I thought I'd die of shock when I saw Mother out there."

"She took it pretty well, though."

"Yeah, she did, didn't she!" I said, surprised.

"She's proud of you."

"You think?" I said.

"Sure of it."

"You know, if I'm going to keep up with this acting stuff, I'm going to have to get over this hang-up I have about being compared with my mother."

"Maybe you should just keep away from acting," he said gravely.

"Not likely!" I said. "Golly, don't you just love it up there? It's like a whole new plane of existence. And fascinating! There's so much to learn. I want to get better and better and better. I'll tell you something—I think I can be *really* good."

"I think you can, too," he said. "I always thought so."

"That's right," I said, grinning at him. "You thought I did a good takeoff on old Isabel. But you know I want to try new, completely different things. I want to experiment. I want to do serious stuff."

"It's hard and dirty work, but somebody's got to do it."

"I think your *joie de vivre* has improved a hundred percent," I said, looking at him critically.

"Some of Tony has rubbed off on me. The next thing you know, I'll be eloping with your mother.

Just kidding. No, actually, I guess I just figure, what the heck. Things keep happening you can't do anything about, so you might as well enjoy the ride. I don't think I've heard the last of Azurée, by the way."

"I thought she was going out West."

"That's what she said. But think about it. She's my mother. She'll be back one of these days, and I don't see how I can just tell her to buzz off. She hasn't had much of a life, you know."

I sighed. "Families."

Heidi purred and, leaving her post by the fire, tiptoed delicately along the furniture and dropped in my lap. "Heidi's the jealous type," I said, scratching her behind the ears. She arched her back and purred loudly.

Tom picked her up gently and dumped her back by the fire, then he sat down again and kissed me. It was much nicer than the stage kiss, warm and close.

I heard Dad's footsteps coming heavily up the hall. Tom looked up, startled.

"That's my father," I said. "Any minute he'll come in here and yell, 'Fourteen years old! What next!'"

"Are you really just fourteen?" said Tom.

"My birthday's next week," I said quickly.

"You look older."

"You should see me with a pewter rinse on my hair."

"No, thanks," said Tom. "I like your hair just the way it is."

I had sort of lost my taste for pewter rinses myself, but I remembered that if it hadn't been for Moonlight Madness, there was a chance I would never have come to Hendleyville, which would have been too bad. I certainly hadn't found Hendleyville boring. And then there was Tom . . .

Dad loomed in the doorway. "Don't you kids think it's time we called it a night?" he said.

Tom got up. "I guess I had better be going," he said. "Susy and I were just talking about celebrating her birthday. Maybe we'll go out for dinner or something."

"That's right," said Dad, wrinkling his brow. "Your birthday is next week, isn't it?"

"I'll be fifteen," I said proudly.

"Fifteen!" he groaned. "What next!"

I giggled. There was no pleasing him. He didn't like it when I was fourteen, he didn't like it when I gave sixteen a whirl and now he was complaining about fifteen.

"I'll walk you out to the car," I said to Tom.

I remembered to grab a jacket as we went outside, but it was still cold. Tom put his arm around me to keep warm as we walked out to his car. The car still bore some of the marks of the traffic accident he'd had the night Azurée had come. He ran his fingers over the dent in the fender. "I need to get it over to the body shop," he said. He fingered his healing stitches. "We're all a bit banged up since that accident."

I had no intention of standing in the cold talking about cars. "Look," I said. "We've got a full moon."

Tom looked up. "Funny," he said. "It doesn't look a bit hackneyed to me." He smiled and kissed me.

"I've always admired the moon, don't you remember?" I said weakly.

He smiled at me. "Would you give me your autograph, Miss Howard?"

I fished a ball-point out of the pocket of my jacket and wrote "Susy" with a flourish on the palm of his hand.

He looked at it soberly. "I'll treasure this always," he said.

"Oh, get out of here," I said, grinning.

"Good night, Susy," he said, getting into the car and turning on the ignition.

"Good night," I said softly.

How it happened Janine didn't quite know, but suddenly Craig had shifted to her end of the couch and gathered her up in his arms. His mouth was on hers, warm and soft, and he was pressing her close to him. She was enveloped in the earthy smell of him, of leaves and fresh-cut grass.

An angry voice ripped away the enchantment of their embrace.

"So this is how you take advantage of my absence!"

Janine and Craig tore themselves apart, a shock of guilt replacing the idyllic ecstasy of their kiss. Craig sprang to his feet.

"So this is what I've been paying you for! Goodness knows what's been going on in my own home, right before the eyes of my children! Well, it's happened for the last time! Neither of you needs to come back here again. You'll get your pay in the mail, little as you deserve it, using my home for such carryings-on!"

Love at First Sight
Elaine Harper

BLOSVAL-1-BPA

GUYS, DATING AND OTHER DISASTERS ⬅
by
Arlene Erlbach

My <u>mom died</u> when I was seven. Last year my dad met Joy Kellison, my future stepmother, at a University of Chicago alumni party. They're getting married in a few weeks, and I'm going to be the maid of honor.

Ricky Fingerbaum is my first boyfriend. We haven't exactly experienced 303 blissfully romantic days. He has never whispered sweet anythings in my ear or even sent me a valentine.

As soon as I wake up, I hear the phone ring. "Henny!" my father calls. "This one is a real looney tune! He wants to talk to his *beautiful wife*. Can't you find a normal boy to date at that high school?"

All excerpts from GUYS, DATING AND OTHER DISASTERS.

LOU DUNLOP STRIKES AGAIN!

More about that "fearless" teen detective and his sexy
sidekick, Jessie. This time Jessie is in hot water, and it's
up to Lou to bail her out.

"This is the life, Jes, the sun and the water,
and nothing to do but enjoy them," I said.

"I'm glad you could come along, Lou. I
really didn't think your father would let you.
Didn't he say he wanted you to work all
summer?"

"Well, I just convinced him that a guy
needed a break before starting his senior year
in high school. We've got two whole weeks to
drown ourselves in pleasure."

"Drown might be an unfortunate expression
at the seashore...."

Is Jessie more right than she knows?

Read all about it in *Cliffhanger* by Glen Ebisch, coming
in July from Crosswinds.

NOW YOU CAN GET ALL THE FIRST LOVE BOOKS YOU MISSED.... WHILE QUANTITIES LAST!

To receive these FIRST LOVE books,
complete the order form for
a minimum of two books,
clip out and send together with
check or money order
payable to Silhouette Reader Service
(include 75¢ postage and handling) to:

In the U.S.:
901 Fuhrmann Blvd.
P.O. Box 1397
Buffalo, NY 14240

In Canada:
P.O. Box 609
Fort Erie, Ontario
L2A 5X3

QUANTITY	BOOK #	ISBN #	TITLE	AUTHOR	PRICE
☐	129	06129-3	The Ghost of Gamma Rho	Elaine Harper	$1.95
☐	130	06130-7	Nightshade	Jesse Osborne	1.95
☐	134	06134-X	Killebrew's Daughter	Janice Harrell	1.95
☐	135	06135-8	Bid for Romance	Dorothy Francis	1.95
☐	136	06136-6	The Shadow Knows	Becky Stewart	1.95
☐	137	06137-4	Lover's Lake	Elaine Harper	1.95
☐	138	06138-2	In the Money	Beverly Sommers	1.95
☐	139	06139-0	Breaking Away	Josephine Wunsch	1.95
☐	143	06143-9	Hungarian Rhapsody	Marilyn Youngblood	1.95
☐	144	06144-7	Country Boy	Joyce McGill	1.95
☐	145	06145-5	Janine	Elaine Harper	1.95
☐	146	06146-3	Call Back Yesterday	Doreen Owens Malek	1.95

QUANTITY	BOOK #	ISBN #	TITLE	AUTHOR	PRICE
☐	147	06147-1	Why Me?	Beverly Sommers	$1.95
☐	161	06161-7	A Chance Hero	Ann Gabhart	1.95
☐	166	06166-8	And Miles to Go	Beverly Sommers	1.95
☐	169	06169-2	Orinoco Adventure	Elaine Harper	1.95
☐	171	06171-4	Write On!	Dorothy Francis	1.95
☐	172	06172-2	The New Man	Carrie Lewis	1.95
☐	173	06173-0	Someone Else	Becky Stuart	1.95
☐	174	06174-9	Adrienne and the Blob	Judith Enderle	1.95
☐	175	06175-7	Blackbird Keep	Candice Ransom	1.95
☐	176	06176-5	Daughter of the Moon	Lynn Carlock	1.95
☐	178	06178-1	A Broken Bow	Martha Humphreys	1.95
☐	181	06181-1	Homecoming	Elaine Harper	1.95
☐	182	06182-X	The Perfect 10	Josephine Wunsch	1.95
☐	185	06185-4	Stop Thief!	Francis Dorothy	1.95
☐	187	06187-0	Birds of A Feather	Janice Harrell	1.95
☐	188	06188-9	Tomorrow and Tomorrow	Brenda Cole	1.95
☐	189	06189-7	Ghost Ship	Becky Stuart	1.95

Your Order Total $ _____

☐ (Minimum 2 Book Order)
Add appropriate sales tax $ _____

Postage and Handling   .75

I enclose   _____

Name _____

Address _____

City _____

State/Prov. _____ Zip/Postal Code _____

FL-RO2B

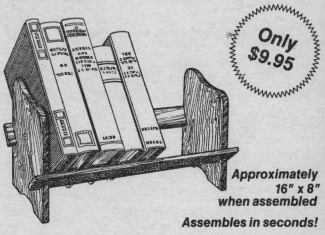